THE HASHTAG HUNT

KRISTINA SEEK

Ebook formatting by Champagne Book Design
Cover design by Liam Ashurst
Editing by Twin Tweaks Editing

Visit the author's website at www.kristinaseek.com

DEDICATION

For my mom, who is my biggest fan.

&

In memory of Amy Virginia Mohler,
who brought joy and laughter to all who knew her.

CHAPTER ONE

Lauren

LAUREN TAPPED HER BEER BOTTLE AGAINST HER BEST FRIEND'S martini. "To Ivy, for knowing where to find a man bun."

"To hipster baristas!" Ivy raised her glass and returned the clink. "And to my girl Lauren, for being another hashtag closer to ten grand."

"Cheers to us!" They enjoyed the first sip of their drinks, and the laid-back atmosphere of Barkley's Pub was what Lauren needed to catch her breath. It had been over two hours since she started hunting hashtags, and she knew she'd be at it for several more hours if all went well. She picked up the menu on the table and said, "I should eat something while we're waiting."

"Let's split something we can eat in a hurry," Ivy suggested as she set her martini down on the high-top table. "Once you get the text, we'll have to book it out of here, right?"

"Right." Lauren drank more of her IPA. "But only if the photo is accepted. If it's not, I'm out, and we can take our sweet time eating all the comfort food Barkley's has to offer." She grabbed her phone off the table and reopened the #HashtagHunt app. Her wide grin waned. "No news yet. I'm still in fourth place."

"Out of how many people?"

"Lots." Lauren's smile returned. "Over a thousand people signed up, and there are around six hundred still in it."

"And you're in fourth place?!"

"I hope I can stay in the running with the next one. There's no telling what I'll have to find." The friends read the menu, debated their options, and settled on the fried pickles. After they ordered, Ivy leaned forward. "Man bun was number four, right?"

"Right. Eight to go. I'm in for a long night."

"Seems like an easy way to win ten thousand dollars."

"I thought so too, but nothing about this has been easy," Lauren said. "Which is why your drinks and pickles are on me. Finding the man bun so fast must have helped my cause."

"Happy to help," Ivy said as she lifted the olive garnish from her martini. "You'll win the prize money, and Paperback Vinyl will be open for business before you know it."

"From your lips to God's ears, woman."

Ivy took a deep breath. "On the off chance you don't win this contest, let me loan you the money." Lauren rolled her eyes as Ivy kept talking. "It would be a loan, not a gift. You would have to pay me back, but with zero interest." She smiled and tapped the garnish stick against the rim of her glass. "We could have a contract drawn up and everything."

"I love you for offering...again, but my answer will always be, 'No thank you, Ivy.' Doing this on my own is nonnegotiable."

"I know, I know." Ivy shrugged and passed the cocktail stick across the table. "For what it's worth, my offer never leaves the table. A loan, investment, silent partner, whatever."

"I love you too." Lauren accepted the trio of olives and slid the first one off with her teeth. Ivy's grimace made her laugh. "You could hold the olives, you know. Or order a different garnish."

"And deprive my best friend of the world's nastiest snack?" Ivy faked a shocked expression.

"You're the best."

Ivy put her elbows on the table and leaned toward Lauren. "Listen, I heard you about doing this without any help, but what if someone else gets the store on Main Street?"

Lauren's heart ached at the thought, but her brain, as always, course corrected. "Then it wasn't meant to be," she said before she ate the second olive.

"The location and building are perfect."

"Would be a dream come true." Lauren closed her eyes and transformed the eyesore on Main Street in her imagination with ease: retro storefront signage, creative displays of used books and classic albums, vintage record players and turntable stands sold on consignment. Despite the positive feedback on her market research and a rock-solid business plan, she could not renovate the building or stock her store without some serious cash flow. Lauren lacked the collateral to secure a bank loan, and her pride refused to entertain the idea of investors. Her savings account had grown over the years, and if she continued to squirrel away most of her disposable income, she would have the funds to start Paperback Vinyl…in time. A windfall like the Hashtag

Hunt's ten-thousand-dollar grand prize would speed up the loan process.

"If I win this contest in the morning, Main Street could still happen," Lauren said. She ate the last olive, clenched her jaw, and tapped the plastic stick on the table. The server appeared with their food and asked about another round.

Lauren declined. "I need to drive and focus tonight." She looked at the waiter and pointed to Ivy. "She will have another. Hold the olives, please." After the server left, Lauren said, "See? Easy."

"But I like how it looks leaning against the glass." She held up her martini and said, "It looks naked without the olives." Ivy shivered. "I'll never understand how anyone eats the slimy, salty, mushy balls."

"It's because they're delicious, especially with cheese and wine." Lauren lifted a fried pickle and dunked it in ranch sauce.

"Let's agree to disagree," Ivy said before pinching a few pickles off the pile. "Back to the Hashtag Hunt. How did you hear about it, anyway?"

"I saw the link on Twitter," Lauren said. "I spent the morning reading the website, studying the fine print. Signed up on my lunch break, and the first text went out at five o'clock sharp."

"What was it?"

After wiping her greasy fingers on a napkin, Lauren picked up her phone and scrolled through her messages. When she got to the first text from the Wizard, she showed Ivy the screen.

Challenge 1 of 12: #ParachutePants
Time Remaining: 12 hours and 0 minutes

"Parachute pants? Are you kidding me?" Ivy asked. "What did you do?"

"I panicked," Lauren said as she placed her phone back on the table. "Then I figured everyone in the contest would have the same reaction. Believing we were all freaked out calmed me down a bit."

"Parachute pants, though." Ivy stabbed several pickles with her fork. "Did you go to Goodwill or something?"

"I considered that but thought it would take too much time to find something so specific." Lauren opened the app again. Still no change in the leaderboard. "The point is to send a photo as fast as you can, so you get the next hashtag before other players do."

"Right," Ivy said. "Oh, I know! You looked online for a *Teen Beat* cover from the eighties or something."

"I wish." Lauren lowered her phone and looked at Ivy. "The rules are crystal clear: no pictures of pictures, screenshots, staged pictures, Photoshop, using filters or apps. Every photo submitted has to be of something captured in real time. I can crop the photo, but not much else."

"How would they know if you staged something? Or used a filter?"

"Not sure how she does it, but the Wizard booted several people for sending in altered photos."

"She?" asked Ivy. "The Wizard is a she?"

"I think so." Lauren tapped on the Wizard's profile picture on the app and passed the phone to Ivy.

A fair-skinned woman with brunette curls was wearing head-to-toe steampunk: a laced corset embellished with gears and buckles, a ruffled ivory miniskirt worn over tight leather pants, Victorian riding boots, and a felted top hat adorned with vintage goggles. She posed on a mossy rock wall in a field, a carved wooden staff in one hand and an oversized antique lantern in the other.

"What…?" Ivy asked as she used her fingertips to zoom in on the photo. "Is she with the Ren Faire, or is this like the Weird West cosplay we saw at Comicon?"

"I'm not sure, but it's the only photo of the Wizard on the app and website," Lauren said. "Maybe looking like a time-traveling badass while making people jump through hoops for ten grand is her thing."

The waiter set Ivy's second drink on the table and removed her empty glass. Ivy thanked him before asking Lauren, "But what about the parachute pants?" The waiter twitched before he walked away, and they smiled at his confused expression.

"Here, I'll show you," Lauren said as she held out her hand and Ivy placed the phone in her palm. With a few taps of her thumb, Lauren closed out of the app and opened her phone's photo gallery. "I prayed Feral Meryl was still break-dancing for tips. You know how she wears those raggedy black pants with—"

"With all the red zippers!" Ivy squealed.

Lauren nodded. "I drove straight to Center City. Found her by the fountain doing what she does best." Lauren thumbed through her photos. "I took so many photos of her, but this is the one I sent." She handed the phone to Ivy.

The photograph was of an aged African-American woman with deep-set crow's feet and silver dreadlocks. She was break-dancing on a large piece of weathered cardboard. One leg was bent at the knee, and the other was stretched out parallel to the ground as she executed the classic helicopter move. Red zippers were peppered across her black nylon pants.

"Bless it," said Ivy. "Look at her go." She skimmed her fingertips across the screen to zoom in on the image. "Good job getting her busted boom box and tip hat in the picture, too."

"I texted it as fast as I could." Lauren finished her beer. "About five minutes later, I got a text with the next challenge. I checked the app, and I was in eighth place."

Ivy looked up from the phone. "Wait. *Seven people* found parachute pants faster than you?"

"Right?" Lauren twisted the napkin in her lap. "I hope she posts all the photos when the contest is over. I'd love to see how so many people made it past the first challenge."

"Shouldn't you have the next hashtag by now?"

"I'll get it once the Wizard approves the man bun. She's prompt, all things considered. I'm not sure how it's all organized, but it works."

Lauren reopened the #HashtagHunt app on her phone. Nothing new in the standings: @BertieMags in the lead, @JayZeeYou a close second, @ChuckLynn in third, and @Laurenburger hot on their heels. Her smile brightened when she remembered there were over six hundred usernames listed below hers. "Should be any time now."

"Well, I'll help you with as many as I can." Ivy used her phone to check the time. "I have a few hours before I have to go."

"You help like you did with the man-bun photo, I won't let you leave."

"Good luck, my friend," Ivy said. "I have a hot date with Scott Eastwood. Not missing him half-naked in dusty camo, even if you choose to evoke the sacred bestie bylaws. I'm going with Mark to the midnight showing of Scott's new movie."

"Does Mark know your hot date is with Scott Eastwood and not him?"

Ivy jumped in her chair when Lauren's phone vibrated against the table. The text alert rang at full volume, and the screen lit up with a notification. Lauren silently read the newest text message and then passed the phone to Ivy.

Challenge 5 of 12: #HitW (Hottie in the Wild)
Time Remaining: 9 hours and 18 minutes

"Oh, this one is a gimme," Ivy said. "We're in a local bar on a Friday night. There should be hotties as far as the eye can see." She gave the phone back to Lauren and turned in her chair, obviously checking out the male patrons of Barkley's Pub and Pourhouse.

As Ivy looked around, Lauren stared at her phone. She thumbed through the app to the leaderboard. She saw that @BertieMags had fallen to fourth place, moving @JayZeeYou, @ChuckLynn, and Lauren up one position each. She pumped her fist in the air and said, "Yes! Third place!"

"Yaaas, girl!" Ivy turned back to smile at Lauren. "Oh! This is so exciting! Let's find you a hottie so you can take the lead."

Both women stood up, turning their backs to their table. Their eyes passed over the crowd, assessing and dismissing each man in turn. While Lauren did not consider the men unattractive, she thought they fell short of what was probably the Wizard's criteria for a #HitW. If her hottie wasn't hot enough, the photo would be rejected, and she would be out of the contest.

"Oh, look!" said Ivy. "Over by the…um, never mind."

She discreetly pointed with her pinkie finger. "Unless you can crop out the ridiculous shirt."

Lauren looked to where Ivy was pointing. When Lauren saw that the man's gray T-shirt said *Edgy as Heck*, she understood why Ivy was trying not to laugh. "Yeah, he's more of a cutie than a hottie."

They resumed their search, checking out the men playing pool and shooting darts. Lauren prayed an Adonis was primping in the men's room.

"Well," Ivy said, "Barkley's is having an off night. It happens." She did a second sweep of the men playing pool and darts. "I'm sure they all have great personalities, but none of these guys will get you to the next hashtag."

After taking stock of the guys in the areas around their table, Lauren had to agree with Ivy. She reread the text from the Wizard. "The text doesn't say it has to be a guy. The hottie could be a woman. Any bombshells in the house?"

"Besides us, you mean?" Ivy joked. They repeated their sweep of the pub, this time taking inventory of the females. Lauren's shoulders slumped, but the front door creaked open, and a group of women clearly enjoying a girls' night out entered the bar.

Ivy scanned each woman as they walked past the table she was sharing with Lauren. "Yeah. Not to be all shallow, but cougars—or whatever comes after cougars—won't win you this round," she said. "We need some straight-up eye candy."

"Ugh! You're right."

"Should we go back to Port Java?" Ivy asked. "Maybe the poet with the biceps and infinity scarf collection is brooding in his corner."

"Was he there when you found the man bun?"

"No," sighed Ivy. "I may have noticed his favorite wing-back chair was empty. But he could be there now."

"I guess we could try there and the twenty-four-hour gym on Woodlawn," Lauren said. "The owner was on a *GQ* cover a while back. Even if he's not there, we can always scope out the trainers and members. Anyone at the gym on a Friday night must want to be there."

"Sold!" Ivy finished her martini. As she placed the glass on the table, the front door opened again.

Lauren said, "I'll go pay the tab, and we'll be on our way."

Ivy gasped and grabbed Lauren's elbow. "Wait a second…hang on…oh, yes, ma'am! A legit hottie in the wild has entered the building. Holy. Smokes."

Lauren turned around and spotted the newcomer at once. Her knees buckled a bit, and she played it off by quickly plopping down in her chair as she openly stared at him.

"The Wizard will love him," Ivy said as she also sat back down. "He is one card-carrying 'Hottie in the Wild' if ever there was one."

Lauren and Ivy watched him walk their way a few steps before heading to the bar. Instead of getting the bartender's attention, he turned around and leaned his back against the countertop. His eyes narrowed, scanning the room, seeking someone in particular, but his aloof demeanor indicated he'd rather be anywhere else than Barkley's Pub. The slate gray Henley and dark jeans were a great look, in Lauren's opinion. The man was tall and fit with dark hair and dark eyes, by far the most handsome man in the bar. And while Lauren found him attractive, his guarded expression made him unapproachable. Lauren thought he looked like a runway model with a wholesome face and absolute confidence, but with a dark, mysterious quality lurking just beneath the surface.

When the bartender approached him, the hottie turned around, giving Lauren the opportunity to admire his physique from the back. She grabbed her phone off the table and said, "Jackpot."

"Want me to distract him for you?" Ivy asked. "I could spill a drink on his broad shoulders or pretend to flirt with him."

"Pretend?"

"Hey, I'll dig deep and take one for the team," Ivy said with a wink. "Scott Eastwood and Mark will understand I was only helping you get to the next hashtag."

"Friend of the Year over here," Lauren said with a smile. "And interesting how Scott Eastwood always gets top billing." Lauren looked at her friend and shook her head. "Poor Mark."

Ivy rolled her eyes. "It's only our second date, so ease up on the sympathies for Mark." Ivy shrugged one shoulder and said, "He knew I was a stage-five Scott Eastwood fangirl when he asked me to the movies."

Returning her gaze to the hottie, Lauren watched Jess, a scantily clad bartender, stretch across the bar and squeeze his bicep. His back muscles tensed as he stood up straighter, moving his arms out of the bartender's reach. Undeterred, she situated her elbows on the bar, tucked her chin, leaned in close, and peered at him from under her lashes.

"Whoa," said Lauren. "Jess busted out her patented pose in ten seconds flat."

"Then you better hurry," said Ivy. "He's hot, but we don't know if he's smart."

CHAPTER TWO

Brenner

"HEY THERE, SUGAR. WELCOME TO BARKLEY'S," THE bartender said. "It's your first time here, right? I would remember your face," she continued as her gaze raked him from eyes to abs, "and body. How about you pull up a stool so a girl can buy you a drink."

"No thank you." He took a step back and distanced himself from the bar. The woman behind it smoothly rose up from the obviously well-rehearsed pose.

"Hey now, handsome. I'm sorry if I came on too strong, but you're making it kind of hard not to stare." She pulled her shoulders back, and he could easily read her too-tight T-shirt: *Blond Hair. Don't Care.* "You an underwear model or something?"

Before he could answer, Brenner was distracted when a mountain of a man charged the bar and crowded the space beside him. He tore the top sheet off his order pad with a sigh and said, "Got me an eight top out to get white girl wasted." He tilted his head toward a group of women settling into the curved booth in the back corner. Brenner and the bartender looked over and saw a few of the ladies reading the laminated menus, but most of them were scrutinizing the ambiance and patrons of Barkley's. "Now don't flip out on me, but they like their booze fancy." Brenner thought the waiter's baritone voice complemented his ebony skin, bald head, and massive build.

The bartender looked at the drink order. Her rockabilly updo didn't move as she shook her head and laughed. "Anthony, those women walked into a bar with peanut shells on the floor. If they want," her eyes scanned the paper, "roasted cherry bourbon smash and rose petal sangria, they need to sashay their little Botox book club further on down the road." She smacked the paper on the bar and slowly slid it toward Anthony. "Sorry. No can do."

Anthony placed his right hand on his hip as his left hand smacked the drink order. "We may never know why, but those ladies came *here* of all places to have some fun tonight. They sat in my section, and with the new baby and all…" He leaned down, looked her in the eyes, and used one finger to slowly slide the drink order back in front of the bartender. "Do not block my cash flow, woman."

"Okay, Anthony. Calm the hell down." She picked up the order and reread it. "Listen here, I understand cash flow better than anybody, but a…'saffron howler' ain't happening." She rolled her eyes. "Can't they just order the house white like normal women?"

"I'll tell them our blender is broken or something," Anthony said, rising up to his full height. "But you need to make them something fancy…and fast. Don't we have champagne?"

"I have three bottles in the back office, but they're not even cold."

"What about Ol' Man Witer's Moonshine? There are a

few jars left from the playoff parties, right?"

"Good Lord, Anthony," the bartender said with wide eyes. "We're trying to get those rich ladies buzzed, not blind."

"Water it down maybe?"

Pointing a long, red-polished fingernail at the women's table, she said, "You cannot be serious right now, Anthony. You want to serve watered-down hooch to those women?"

"If it can be mixed with other stuff to look expensive and taste delicious, then hell yes I do. Water down the hooch." Anthony reached across the bar and grabbed her by the shoulders. In a low voice, he said, "I'm begging you, boss lady. Please. Think of something."

She turned her gaze from Anthony with a dramatic sigh, and her attention landed back on Brenner at the bar. "What's your name, handsome?"

His eyes went from the bartender to Anthony and back again. "Brenner."

"It's nice to meet you, Brenner. I'm Jess." She reached out to shake his hand, ignoring Anthony tapping his over-sized fingers on the bar. "Mind if I ask your opinion about all this?" she asked, twirling her finger in a circle.

"You want my opinion on what to serve your customers?" Brenner asked.

Anthony pulled out his phone and slumped against the bar, mumbling "Pinterest" under his breath.

"Yeah," Jess said. "What would you add to moonshine to impress people who like elderberries and rose water in their mixed drinks?"

"I drink beer, so I wouldn't know," Brenner said. "If I had to guess, I'd say mixing in ginger ale or lemonade could do the trick. Or maybe a splash of cranberry juice for color?" He nodded his head toward Anthony. "I'd look at what he's finding online and start there."

Jess looked back at Anthony and nodded. "Will do." Returning her eyes back to Brenner, she said, "Can I get you anything to drink while we're consulting Google?"

"Not yet. I'm waiting on a friend," Brenner said. "I'll order something when he gets here."

"Sounds good." She walked away with an exaggerated sway of her hips before looking back over her shoulder to wink at Brenner. "Try not to miss me too much." To Anthony, she said, "Come on back and let's see what's what."

As Anthony rounded the bar to join Jess on the other side, Brenner lowered down onto a bar stool. He pulled his cell phone out of his side pocket to make sure he hadn't missed any calls or texts. "Dammit, Sully," he groaned. "Where are you?"

Brenner's thoughts went back to the meat lover's pizza and Netflix series he had been enjoying a few hours ago. Halfway through an episode, his cell phone chirped from its place on the coffee table. He had planned on ignoring the interruption, but curiosity made him glance at the screen. Scott Sullivan's name was above the word *Stateside*. Brenner lunged toward his phone to pick it up. A second message immediately followed: *Calling in those beers you owe me*.

Instead of texting back, he called his friend and paused the TV show streaming in the background. When Scott answered after the first ring, Brenner said, "Good to hear from you, brother. What's up?"

"Damn, B. I barely put my phone down before you called back like some lovesick airman."

"I either respond to texts right away or two days later. There is no in-between."

"Well, thanks for the rapid reply," Scott said. He cleared his throat and continued. "It's been a while, huh? It's good to hear your voice."

"Yeah, you too."

"What are you up to tonight?"

Brenner leaned back on the sofa and looked at the pile of flattened cardboard boxes ready to sell for a few bucks. "I finished unpacking about an hour ago. Celebrating with a little R and R."

"Rifles and race cars?"

"Not even close," Brenner said with a chuckle.

"Romance and redheads?"

"I wish, brother." Brenner looked around his living room. "I'm eating dinner and watching TV."

"Yeah, no," Scott said. "We can do a lot better than that. You been to Barkley's out on Selwyn yet?"

"Never heard of Barkley's, but then again, I haven't taken the town tour since moving here."

"It's a local bar, low-key. Let's catch up over a bucket of beer and a pool table."

"Yeah...that sounds good." Brenner tried to keep the emotion out of his voice but must have failed.

"Hey now," Scott said. "If you'd rather stay home and finish watching your soap operas, I understand. Rain check?"

"It's good to have you back, Sully."

"I'm texting you the address. See you in thirty."

Scott Sullivan was eleven minutes late. To kill time, Brenner watched Jess and Anthony argue about what to serve the eight top. From his seat at the bar, he overheard "pomegranate syrup" and "sour apple schnapps." He couldn't help but smile.

Anthony showed Jess something on his phone. Jess rolled her eyes as she grabbed ingredients from under the bar. Before long, Jess poured a bright pink concoction out of a cocktail shaker into two shot glasses. Anthony and Jess sampled the drink and agreed they had a winner. Anthony picked up his phone again, and in hushed voices, they argued about garnishes.

"Let's use strawberries and call it a day, Anthony," Jess said as she made a bigger batch of the chosen cocktail. "After a few swallows of Witer's Moonshine, they won't give a crap about what was on the rim of the tumbler."

"Yes! It's *The Anthony and Jess Show!*" said a familiar voice behind Brenner. "Man, some things never change."

Brenner turned around and smiled at his friend. "Sully," he said as he stood up from the stool. "I am so glad to see you, brother."

"You too, kid," Scott said as they went in for a bro hug. Hands clasped. Fists pounded shoulder blades. Brenner tried to swallow around the lump in his throat. The men separated and studied each other.

"Lookin' good, Hollywood," Scott said.

"Wait. Are you seriously taller than me now?" Brenner was incredulous. He looked down at Scott's cowboy boots. He couldn't imagine his friend in lifted shoes, but it was easier to believe than the rumors of his supernatural growth spurt.

"I may have put in a request for modifications here or

there," Scott said with a sly smile. "Gaining a few inches on you was one of the many perks."

"Perks, huh?" Brenner couldn't help but stare at his friend. "I can't believe you're standing in front of me right now."

"Yeah, me either," Scott said with a sigh. "I was beginning to think I'd never see the outside of that hospital."

"Well, growing to six foot six takes time," Brenner said. "I can't wait to hear what tricks those sci-fi legs of yours can do. I heard you're some type of cyborg."

"I can confirm some handy bells and whistles are embedded here and there, and a few features are classified," Scott said. "I'll be using the legs for walking, though. The rest of the mods I won't use."

"Aren't they expecting you to use the tech they gave you for missions, or—"

"No more missions for me," Scott said. "I'm done."

"Done?" Brenner couldn't picture it. Sully had dedicated his life to the Army.

"Honorably discharged." Scott smiled and said, "I'm officially a civilian now."

Brenner was stunned into silence for a few moments. "Then why give you new legs with classified bells and whistles?"

"In a nutshell: a gorgeous genius designed them for a prosthetics company in England." Scott's features softened as he continued. "She heard my story. Talked her bosses into donating some prototypes. She insisted I deserved the biotech as a token of appreciation from allies across the pond, blah blah." He shrugged one shoulder and said, "Another perk."

"The new legs or the gorgeous genius?"

"Yes."

Both men laughed.

"I can't believe you're here," Brenner repeated. He took a deep breath and said, "It took five days to get the word you'd survived. Then another week to hear you were okay."

"Whoever said I was okay is a damn liar," Scott said as they sat down at the bar. "But I don't want to talk about anything heavy. We're relaxing tonight, okay?"

"You got it. Nothing heavy."

Jutting his chin toward Jess and Anthony, Scott asked, "What were those two squawking about when I walked up?"

Brenner tilted his head toward the eight top and said, "The entire table ordered cocktails off the menu."

Scott glanced at the women and then watched Anthony approach their table with several pink drinks on a tray. "Yeah, they don't look like they're here to split a pitcher of Milwaukee's Best."

The men's laughter caught Jess's attention and she looked behind her. "Sully!" The sway was still on her hips, and she was wiping her hands with a bar towel. "I heard you were headed back this way. Welcome home, my handsome hero."

"Darling Jess," Scott said, and he reached for her hand. After he kissed her knuckles, he said, "How about a couple Dos Equis for me and my friend here."

"Sure thing, but for the record: all your beers are on the house, Sully. Forever," Jess said as she popped the tops off the bottles and put lime wedges on the rims. "Your money is no good here."

"And the perks. Just. Keep. Coming!" Scott laughed and

nodded toward Brenner. "What about his money? Is it any good here?"

"Well, the jury's still out," she said as she passed each man a beer. "Brenner and I only recently became acquainted. Is he a brave war hero like you?"

"You bet. Braver, even."

Brenner started to dispute the claim, but Scott spoke over his voice. He angled the neck of his beer bottle toward Brenner and said, "Brenner here has a pile of shiny medals. A few are for the day he saved my life."

"Not at all what happened, and you know it," Brenner said as he shook his head. "The docs saved your life, Sully. I got you to the bird, but once you were on it, it was all them."

"Well, it sounds like you moved him from where he got hurt to where he got help," Jess said. She tapped her nails on the bar top. "Therefore, your drinks are always on the house too, handsome."

"Easy, tiger; 'handsome' here already has a sweetheart…and it's gotten serious." Cutting his eyes toward Brenner, Scott said, "Right? It's serious between you two?"

"Oh…um, yeah." Brenner made a mental note to thank Scott for the white lie as soon as Jess was out of earshot. "It's very serious."

Jess pouted.

"Tonight's a guys' night, otherwise his woman would be sitting in his lap about now," Scott said. Brenner tried to make eye contact with Scott so he could silently plead, "Dial it down a notch," but Scott was focused on Jess.

"Okay, yeah. Okay, that makes sense," Jess said while she patted her hair. "Thought I was losing my touch for a minute there."

"Impossible," said Scott. "Poor Brenner here has it bad for his girlfriend. Blinded to all other beauty in the world."

"Well, she's a lucky girl," Jess raised an eyebrow and said, "and you should tell her I said so."

"Thank you. I will." Brenner cleared his throat. In an attempt to change subjects, he asked, "So, how did your fancy cocktails turn out?"

"Well, the good news is they're going to make it," Jess said with an eye roll. "We mixed flat Cherry 7UP and a mason jar of the shine. Doctored it up a bit with a little of this and that. Their first round was on the house to soften the blow of Barkley's being fresh out of candied ginger peels."

"I'm sorry," Scott said. "What now?"

Jess and Brenner glanced toward the party of eight. Most seemed to enjoy Jess's pink drink, but a few were thumbing through their phones. To Brenner, it looked like they were searching for another bar.

"If they stay for another round, I'll be sure to over-charge them, so they feel better about—" Jess stopped talking and stared over Brenner's right shoulder. "You are famous!" she shouted. "I knew it! Were you in a movie or something before joining the Army?"

Scott laughed as Brenner choked on his beer. "Who, me? Not at all." Brenner looked at Scott and then back to Jess. "Why would you ask me that?"

She pointed a finger and said, "Because that woman over there is taking your picture like there's no tomorrow."

Brenner and Scott followed Jess's gaze and looked directly at the woman the same moment her phone's flash went off.

CHAPTER THREE

Lauren

"**O**h, crap," Lauren gasped. She ducked her head, darted into the narrow hallway, and headed straight toward the bathrooms. Grateful to find the ladies' room empty, Lauren locked herself in a stall and fired off a text to Ivy.

Lauren: OMG. So busted. Big time.

Ivy: U ok?

Lauren: Nope!

Lauren sent Ivy the last picture she had taken with her phone. The hottie's torso was turned toward the camera, and there was no mistaking his startled reaction: eyebrows lifted high, eyelids jolted wide, and jaw dropped low. His friend on the left was curious enough to lean back on his stool to look in her direction. His expression was confused, yet pleasant. And behind the bar was Jess. Her fiery glare, snarled lip, and pointed finger conveyed her utter disdain of the situation.

Lauren watched three dots bounce as Ivy typed her reply. The dots disappeared and then reappeared.

Ivy: OMG! There are TWO hotties now?

Lauren leaned against the stall door, counted to ten, and sent another text.

Lauren: Please come here before Jess does.

Ivy: Yeah, girl, she looks PISSED… Sit tight. On my way.

Focusing on the task at hand, Lauren took a deep breath and pressed the home button on her phone. She opened the camera roll app and said to herself, "Eyes on the prize, woman." She hadn't realized how many pictures she had taken from various darkened hiding spots around the bar until she found her first photo and considered the shots in order. The hottie's facial expressions varied as she scrolled through the images: unease when Jess was flirting, bewilderment as Jess and Anthony debated a drink order, pensiveness when he sat alone at the bar, surprise at his friend's arrival.

The next photo captured unfiltered joy as he greeted his friend. The huge smile suited him, and the dimples were a pleasant surprise. Lauren made fast work of cropping the friend and Jess out of the picture and sending it to the Wizard. She opened the app, and @Laurenburger was still in third place. She hoped @ChuckLynn and @JayZeeYou were still struggling to find a #HitW, wherever they were.

Lauren heard the bathroom door open and her friend's voice. "Lauren?"

"In here." Lauren cracked open the stall door. After confirming the coast was clear, she opened the door the rest of the way and walked out of the stall.

"Girl, what happened?" Ivy walked straight to the sink and placed her purse on the countertop.

"He started smiling, and I got greedy…and sloppy, I guess." She joined Ivy at the sink and met her friend's eyes in the mirror. "I am so embarrassed."

"Did you get a decent picture of him before they busted you?"

"Yes." Lauren found the photo on her phone and turned the screen toward Ivy. "Here's what I sent." Ivy whistled when she saw the picture and took the phone from Lauren. "I think the dimples make him especially Wizard-worthy."

After pinching and pulling the image to enlarge it, Ivy said, "Well done, you. When did you send it?"

"Less than a minute ago."

"This man is going to get you to the next hashtag." Ivy returned the phone to Lauren and looked at her reflection in the mirror above the sink. "Does his friend have dimples?" she asked while pulling her makeup bag out of her purse.

"Um, I don't think so. Not that I could see anyway." Lauren put her phone in her back pocket and yanked the elastic out of her hair. She smoothed back the flyaways around her face before returning her long locks to the messy bun she'd been wearing since she left work.

"I didn't even notice the friend walk in or join him. I was catching up on Instastories." With a heavy sigh, she said, "I need to put my phone down more often. Can't believe I missed him walking in." She found her trusty Bombshell Berry lip gloss in her makeup bag and applied it.

Lauren pulled her Cherry ChapStick from her front pocket and laughed when Ivy rolled her eyes. "Was Jess still behind the bar?"

"Yeah, I overheard her saying something about needing more 7UP." Ivy rubbed her lips together to even out the shine. "Something about making the next round less lethal."

Lauren pocketed her ChapStick and turned to watch Ivy finish primping. With a hip against the sink, she asked, "Are the guys still at the bar?"

While finger-combing her honey-blond hair, Ivy said, "They were when I walked by to come in here."

Lauren watched as Ivy fished in her makeup bag and pulled out a mascara comb. After she straightened her lashes and smoothed her eyebrows, she checked herself out in the mirror one last time. "Alright, so want to make a beeline for the front door?"

Before Lauren could answer, three women entered the ladies' room. She recognized them from the group who had entered the bar when she was searching for a female #HitW.

"I told you this hole in the wall would be a good time," said one woman as she stumbled into a stall. She hiccupped and then said, "And how adorable are those two fellas sitting at the bar? Where have they been my whole life?"

"Well, they weren't even alive for the first half of it," said a voice from another stall.

"Daaaamn, Margot," said the woman leaning against the wall as she waited her turn. "Moonshine makes you mean."

"I'm not mean, I'm honest," Margot said before unleashing a lengthy, loud, masculine belch. "And slightly less refined."

"Nice one, Margot," said Ivy as she opened the bathroom door. "Have fun storming the castle!"

As the door closed behind them, Ivy and Lauren heard Margot shout, "As you wish!"

Lauren stopped on the other side of the door and said, "Okay, so I'll pay the tab, and then we'll go somewhere far,

far from here to see if I get another hashtag."

"Sounds like a solid plan. Follow me until we reach our table," Ivy said. "And whatever you do, don't look at him."

"Right. Got it."

They left the hallway, and Lauren made it five steps before she risked a glance toward the bar. Her #HitW was staring right at her. She faltered the moment their eyes met, and his expression changed from confusion to concern. Her heart skipped a beat, and she came to a sudden stop.

Ivy was a few steps ahead and whirled around when Lauren gasped. "I told you not to look at him!" she hissed.

"I know, I know," Lauren whispered, breaking her eye contact with him to look at Ivy. "I'm sorry. Let's keep going."

They continued toward their table when the hottie's friend slid off his bar stool and approached them. "Hello!" he said with a friendly wave. "Hold up."

This time it was Ivy who stumbled before halting her retreat. Lauren nearly slammed into her but avoided a collision by swerving to the left. She placed her hand on Ivy's back and gently pushed forward, hoping to resume their exit.

"Please don't go," the man said with a smile. "I come in peace."

"We're on our way out," Ivy said, looking him up and down. "Shame, really."

"No, please stay. I'd love to buy you a drink." With a wink, he said, "You could tell me all about the time your friend took a picture of my friend and nobody knew why."

Lauren watched the hottie leave his stool and walk their way. "It's kind of a long story, and we have to go," she said. When he joined them in the middle of the bar, she forced herself to look him in the eyes. "I didn't mean any trouble."

"Hey, no harm done," he replied. "Curious is all."

Jess walked out from behind the bar, stood next to the guys and said, "Yes, I'm also curious why you were taking his picture. We don't allow flash photography of our patrons on the premises!"

"Since when?" Ivy said, pointing to several discolored Polaroid pictures stapled to the wall behind them. "Wet T-shirt contests and keg stands are cool, but one accidental cell phone snap is against Barkley's corporate culture? Please."

"Those people," Jess said as she gestured toward the photos, "posed for the camera, honey." She rested her other hand on the hottie's bicep. "This gentleman had no idea you were stalking in the shadows."

A gasp went up from eavesdroppers. "I'm not a stalker!" Lauren said to the people who had heard Jess's claim. "I've never seen this guy before tonight." She looked at the hottie and said, "Right?"

"Right. We haven't met," he said. He respectfully studied Lauren's face. "I would remember you."

"Can't blame the girl for taking his picture," said one woman sitting near the bar. Fanning her face with her hand, she drawled, "He's so handsome."

The hottie ducked his head, but not before Lauren saw him blush.

Margot and her friends returned from the ladies' room, and Lauren watched as one of the ladies who had stayed at the table filled her friends in on what they'd missed. Margot said, "That is adorable. Let's all get a picture with him!" She tried to tug a few of her friends out of their chairs. "Come on! Get up!"

"Okay, she's cut off," Jess said. "There's not enough Cherry 7UP in the world to save her."

One of the women at the table refused Margot's efforts to get a group shot. She smacked Margot's hands away and looked directly at Lauren, "So why did you take his picture, honey?"

"I think we all want to know," said Jess. A din of agreement rose from the other people beginning to take an interest in the conversation.

The man's friend spoke up. "Out of curiosity, why didn't you take my picture?"

"Your friend got here first," Ivy replied with a shrug. "And our mission is time sensitive."

"Your mission?" he asked, standing up straighter. By now, everyone in earshot had tuned in to the discussion.

"Yes, our mission," Ivy insisted to the crowd. "What, two grown-ass women can't be on a mission?" she asked the people listening to her.

"Of course they can," said the hottie's friend. "Women conduct recon and OPSEC on covert, classified, time-sensitive missions all day, every day." He took another step closer and said, "So what's your name, soldier?"

"I'm Ivy. This is Lauren," she said, nodding to her friend.

Copying her nod, he said, "Brenner." Placing his hand on his own chest, he said, "I'm Scott."

"Scott?" Ivy startled a bit. "Huh. Great name."

"Brenner," said Lauren. Realizing she had spoken aloud while staring at him, she played it off by saying, "I'm sorry about taking your picture without your permission, but I swear it was important."

"Important because it was for your mission?" he asked.

Lauren nodded her head. "I know it sounds crazy."

"We can help," Scott said. "We kick ass at missions. Even the crazy ones." He looked at Brenner. "Well, except the one time."

Brenner dismissed Scott's comment with a wave of his hand. "I would like to know why your mission needed my picture."

"Oh, this ought to be good," Jess said to a few customers next to her. She plopped down in an empty chair at a table and crossed her legs.

"Excuse us a minute," said Ivy as she huddled close to Lauren. With their backs turned to most of the crowd, she whispered, "Explain you needed a picture of a hot...er, a handsome guy. You'll make his day, promise."

"No way!" hissed Lauren. "One: too embarrassing, and two: he'd never believe me."

"Show him the website, the tweet, the app, the texts," said Ivy. "He'll know it's a real contest, and he'll be flattered."

Their heads were bent low as they whispered to each other. Around them, soft murmurs filled the bar as people discussed theories. Everyone jumped when Anthony yelled from the back, "Jess!" He stomped across the bar to her and barked, "Order up!"

"Okay, but it's going to be a minute," said Jess. She stood on her chair and announced to all the people in Barkley's, "The bar is closed until this mess gets sorted."

Murmurs escalated to mutterings, sprinkled with groans and boos.

"Freaking tell him before there's a riot," Ivy hissed at

Lauren. "We'll belly-laugh about the hottie hashtag embarrassment while you deposit ten thousand dollars in the bank."

"Ugh, okay. Okay!" They broke their huddle and Lauren took a lungful of air. She spoke to Brenner and all in one breath said, "I'm in a photo contest, and it's more of a scavenger hunt than a mission." She cut her eyes to Ivy. "I'm taking pictures as fast as I can and sending them to the judge. You were in the right place at the right time."

"You entered the picture you snuck in a photo contest?" Jess asked.

Lauren was mortified. Trying to keep the defensiveness out of her voice, she said, "Yes, and I did it because I had to."

Brenner asked Lauren, "You sent my picture somewhere?" When she nodded, he said, "I'm not upset, but I would like to know where it went."

"The photo contest is called the Hashtag Hunt." Lauren moved closer to Brenner and opened the app on her phone. "I needed a picture of a man."

Brenner looked at the screen and then swept his eyes across the room. "There are dozens of men here. Why did you choose me?"

"Um," Lauren cleared her throat. "I noticed you while you were sitting at the bar."

"Well," said Scott, "I was also sitting at the bar."

"Not at first," said Ivy. "You arrived after he did, right?"

"Noticed that, did you?" Scott looked at Ivy with a raised eyebrow.

Ivy shrugged and then turned to Lauren. "Tell him the rest so we can get out of here."

"I needed a picture of an attractive guy...in a public

place. A hot guy…" Lauren stammered.

"Or, as the kids today call it: 'a hottie in the wild,'" said Ivy.

"A hottie in the wild?" asked Jess.

"I needed a photo of one, as fast as possible…and you walked in as we were about to leave. So I took your picture," Lauren said to Brenner.

"Why not ask me if you could take my picture for your contest?" Brenner asked.

"It has to be a candid shot, no posing allowed," said Lauren. "If I break the rules, I'm disqualified."

"I'm sorry. Are you saying 'hottie?' 'In the wild?'" Scott didn't hide his confusion. "That's not a thing, is it?"

"Oh yeah," Ivy said. "It's a thing. My Facebook friends post pictures of hot guys out in public all the time. Subways, airports, Disney World, construction sites, tattoo parlors, in line for coffee, carpool…" she trailed off with a shrug. "Wherever."

"Are you serious?" Scott looked at Brenner and said, "I'm not sure men could get away with a 'Honey in the Wild' Facebook group."

"Please, Scott. We ladies are making up for lost time," said Ivy. "A handful of hotties on Facebook doesn't compare to the tons of T & A on the Internet."

All who heard Ivy's voice nodded, and Margot shouted, "Preach!"

"Okay. Let me see if I understand what you're saying," Jess said as she sat up straighter in her chair. "Women take and post pictures of hot men they see out and about in town."

"All. Day," confirmed Ivy.

Jess left her chair and went behind the bar. She bent

down and then reappeared, plopping her oversized purse on the bar top. She fished her phone out of the bag. "Show me the way."

"Get on Facebook." Ivy walked over to Jess. "I got you."

Lauren looked at Brenner. Pointing to Ivy and Jess at the bar, she said, "I did not take your picture for that Facebook group. I needed it for this contest, I swear."

Brenner said, "I'm flattered you found me attractive enough for your photo."

"I knew it!" Ivy shouted from the bar. She looked up from Jess's phone. "I told her any normal guy would love knowing he was a hottie in the wild."

"Well," said Jess, looking at her phone, "Facebook just got a hell of a lot better." Lauren watched her move her thumb across the screen. "And these guys have no idea these pictures are being taken?"

"Plenty of women get caught," Ivy said with a pointed look toward Lauren. "Most play it off by pretending they're texting someone or taking a selfie. A friend of mine once acted like she was looking for a coupon when she was busted in line at Dick's Sporting Goods."

Jess looked up from her phone and said, "And some women run away and hide in the ladies' room."

"Take it easy on her," Brenner said to Jess. He turned his attention to Lauren and said, "It's worth it if the picture helped you win the contest." When Lauren didn't respond, he asked, "Did you win?"

"The contest doesn't end until tomorrow. I have to take twelve pictures, and yours was number five," Lauren responded. "If your picture is accepted, I'll get a text with instructions for number six."

"And if it's not accepted?" Brenner asked.

"Then I'm out of the contest. First contestant to have twelve pictures approved before the deadline wins."

"Wins what?" the crowd asked.

"Ten thousand dollars," said Lauren. There were whistles and exclamations as the majority of the people around them picked up their phones.

"What's the app called again?" asked Margot.

"You had to register by noon today, and the contest started at five o'clock." The crowd grumbled, and most put their phones down.

"When's the deadline?" asked Jess.

Lauren said, "Five in the morning. Twelve hours to send in twelve pictures."

Anthony was looking at his phone and asked, "Are you BertieMags?"

"No. Laurenburger. I'm in third place."

Anthony looked at the screen. "Says here, Laurenburger's in second place." He turned his wrist to show the people standing next to him.

"Wait, what?" Lauren pulled up the standings on her phone to see for herself. Ivy left Jess at the bar to join Lauren. Together, they looked at the screen. In first place was @JayZeeYou, @Laurenburger in second, and @BertieMags had risen from fourth to third place.

"Second place!" Ivy shouted as she hugged Lauren. The crowd cheered and raised their drinks, celebrating the victory.

Lauren was still staring at the leaderboard when a text notification from the Wizard appeared on the top of her screen. "I got the next hashtag!" She closed out of the app and opened her messages. "Wait, what?"

The shock must have been evident on her face because Ivy looked down at Lauren's phone. "Hold up," Ivy said. "Is this a joke?"

Lauren groaned.

"What's your next photo assignment?" asked Jess as she returned to her chair. "Sexy lumberjacks? Eight-pack abs?"

"Ugh," said Ivy. "If only."

CHAPTER FOUR

Brenner

BRENNER STOOD DUMBFOUNDED BY THE INTERACTIONS between Lauren, Ivy, Jess, Anthony, the women enjoying their girls' night out, and others scattered throughout the bar. Leaning over to Scott, he said in a low voice, "This place is crazy."

"Yeah, Barkley's is in rare form tonight." Scott gestured to the people around them and said, "But, you gotta admit, this beats the hell out of binge-watching Hallmark movies…or whatever you hotties watch when not out in the wild."

Brenner rolled his eyes before cutting them to Scott. "You know, I'm not convinced this isn't one of your infamous pranks," he said, shaking his head. "Like pepper spray in the Humvee's air vents."

Scott leaned his head back and laughed. "Classic." He slapped Brenner on the back and said, "I thought you'd never stop coughing."

"Me either." Brenner couldn't help but smile. "Jackass."

"Good times." Scott pretended to wipe tears from his eyes. "Listen, brother, I'm good, but not 'create a fake app everyone can download' good."

"I don't know…you've had a lot of downtime lately." Brenner laughed. "Maybe your brilliant genius in London set this up for you months ago. Another perk, right?"

"Wrong." Scott looked down at his phone. "This contest is legit, and she is sitting pretty in second place."

Sitting pretty is right, Brenner thought to himself. Earlier, when Lauren explained why she took his picture, he was too distracted by her natural beauty to grasp her explanation. She wore minimal, if any, makeup while casually dressed in jeans and a T-shirt. It was hard to tell how long her hair was because it was in one of those messy buns women knot up in under five seconds. Lauren had clearly been embarrassed and nervous as she explained the contest, as though she didn't want any attention. Either she didn't know she was gorgeous, or she knew and didn't care.

Brenner and Scott were among many in the bar who corroborated Lauren's story with a quick Google search. The official Hashtag Hunt website confirmed the contest rules and ten-thousand-dollar grand prize. The leaderboard stated @Laurenburger was in second place, and once it was evident her "HitW" entry had been approved, Brenner appreciated her honesty. He was impressed by Lauren's success, especially considering hundreds of "hashtag hunters" were competing. Brenner found her intelligence and initiative even more attractive than her good looks.

Noticing the women were no longer celebrating Lauren's second-place status, Brenner and Scott approached them. "What's the matter?" Scott asked. "Did you get your next mission?"

"Oh, we got it," Ivy said. "Unfortunately."

Lauren looked Ivy in the eyes. "Listen, you found the

man bun and the hottie," she said, nodding her head at Brenner. "You're why I'm in second place. I would never ask or expect you to help with this."

"Help with what?" asked Scott.

Lauren lifted her phone and showed the men her most recent text from the Wizard.

Challenge 6 of 12: #DumpsterDiveFind
Time Remaining: 8 hours and 21 minutes

"You have to find something in a dumpster?" Brenner asked.

"What? Gross." Margot was eavesdropping from her table. To her friends, she said, "Not as fun as finding a hottie." Her seven friends nodded in agreement.

"It's pretty much the polar opposite of finding a hottie," said Ivy.

"I'm not thrilled about it either," Lauren said as she grabbed Ivy's hands. "But, I'm almost halfway through this crazy contest, and I'm in second place, Ivy." She squeezed Ivy's hands. "Second. Place."

"I know, girl," said Ivy. "And we need to hustle so you can take the lead and make Paperback Vinyl happen." Her fingers squeezed back. "But I call dibs on shining my torch app from a safe distance."

"You're a wonderful person."

"Only sometimes," Ivy said. "I'd like to go on record as stating that hashtag number six is nasty."

"No arguments here," said Lauren.

"And dangerous," Ivy added.

"Well, it could be, yes. We'll have to be careful."

"And illegal."

"Huh… Yeah, probably. We'll avoid the ones with security cameras."

"You know, I've been dumpster diving a time or two," said Anthony as he dragged his thumb across his phone's screen. "Avoid anywhere with 'Private Property' or 'No Trespassing' signs. It's not all bad if you know which dumpsters to search."

"He's right," said a man sitting at Jess's table. "I found some stereo speakers and a DVD player in the dumpster behind my apartment. They cleaned up good as new."

"Good as new?" repeated Ivy. "Really?"

"Well, one of the speakers was banged up a bit," he said. "But the wife put a potted plant on top so you can't see the scratches."

"Look, zero dollars is a price most people can't resist," Anthony said with a shrug. He waved his phone back and forth. "Don't knock it. Dumpster diving's another type of scavenger hunt if you think about it."

"It's like my consignment stores and Goodwill," said Margot. "Guess how much this dress cost."

"Five bucks," said everyone at her table.

"You bet your sweet candy asses! Five bucks for this White House Black Market dress originally priced for a hundred and seven dollars." Raising her pink moonshine in the air, she said, "Thou shalt never pay retail! And all the people said…"

"Amen!" said the crowd.

While they were cheering, Brenner asked Lauren, "Can I see the text again?" He looked at the screen and said, "So you have to take a picture of a dumpster dive find, but you don't necessarily have to find it yourself, right?"

Lauren reread the text and gave it some thought. "I

guess so. But—"

"And does a 'find' have to be a nice item?" Jess asked. "It sounds like you just have to find something in a dumpster."

"Now hang on," said Anthony. "It's common knowledge 'dumpster dive find' means 'cash in the trash.'" To Lauren, he said, "If your challenge is to photograph a 'find,' it needs to be a picture of something valuable."

"But isn't 'valuable' subjective?" asked Ivy. To the man at Jess's table, she asked, "What's your name?"

"Dave."

"No offense, Dave, but if I see a DVD player in a dumpster, I'm leaving it there."

Margot snapped her fingers and said, "Hey, barkeep!" When Jess looked up from her phone, Margot said, "You have a dumpster behind this bar, right?" Jess nodded. Margot leaned across the table and asked, "Did you throw away anything expensive today?"

Jess returned her attention to her phone, and if Brenner had to guess, she was still scrolling through hotties on Facebook. She said, "Sorry, but I prefer to keep my expensive things out of the dumpster behind the bar."

A woman sitting next to Margot asked Lauren, "What if we throw something nice away and you pretend to find it?"

"That's cheating," said Anthony. He must have been thumbing through the app because he said, "It's right here in the rules: 'Participants will be removed from the Hashtag Hunt if photos are manipulated, staged, or affected by the photographer in any way. Any posed or constructed image submitted as a "found moment" is cause for immediate disqualification.'"

"Damn, girl," said Jess. "They're making you work for

the ten grand, huh?"

"They're not just giving it away, no." Lauren took a few steps toward the door. "And I want to win that money, so I need to start looking through dumpsters."

"I'm right behind you," Ivy said, returning her phone to her purse. "Let's roll."

They only made it a few steps toward the exit before Scott shouted, "Now hang on!" He walked up to Ivy and said, "While I am loving the little black dress and strappy heels, dumpster diving calls for long sleeves, thick pants, and big boots. Even if you're on lighting detail."

"I'll be going in the dumpsters," Lauren said, looking down at her blue jeans and red Chucks. "I'll be careful."

Scott appraised Lauren's attire and asked, "Have any thick gloves? A pocketknife? Eye protection?"

Lauren shook her head. "No…but we can stop at a store."

"You don't have time for stores." Scott looked at Brenner and asked, "Your ruck handy?"

"Yeah." Brenner looked at Lauren while nodding toward Scott. "I hate to admit it, but he's right. You'll need safety gear, supplies, and more light than a smartphone's torch app will give you." With a smile, he said, "I'd hate for you to win ten grand but spend thirty grand on hospital bills because of a staph infection."

Scott said, "And Ivy can't hold the flashlight, be the lookout, and start the car if you need to make a fast getaway."

Brenner saw Lauren and Ivy exchange nervous looks.

"We'll figure it out on the way," Ivy said.

Brenner wanted Lauren to succeed but agreed with Scott. Attempting a challenge like this without a plan was risky. "On the way to where?" he asked.

"Not sure yet," Lauren said. "Ivy can Google 'dumpster diving' while I drive around. We'll see what turns up."

"Way ahead of you," Ivy said, waving her phone in the air.

Brenner looked at Anthony and asked, "Any advice on where they'd find something good enough?"

"Well, off the top of my head," Anthony said, rocking back on his heels, "either behind those ritzy condos on Morrison or Harbour's Marketplace on Colony. All the shops in the building use the same dumpster."

"What about the mall?" asked Ivy.

"Way too much security," Anthony said. "Low-key is key."

"I'll second looking through the trash bin next to Harbour's," Dave said. "Last year, I found a fancy pocketbook with a busted zipper. Still had the price tag on it and paper stuffing inside and everything." To Ivy, he said, "Can you believe they wanted two hundred and seventy-five dollars for a purse?"

Ivy asked, "Do you remember the brand?"

He held up his thumb and pointer finger about an inch apart. "The little bitty logo said 'Kate Spade.'" Ivy gasped. He held up his hands two feet apart. "Big ole bucket of a purse too."

Jess said, "If I spent serious money on a purse and the freaking zipper didn't work, heads would roll."

"Some of the teeth on the zipper were bent. I fixed it with some needle-nose pliers and elbow grease," he said. "Gave it to the wife for Christmas, and she about had a heart attack."

"Did you tell her you found it in a dumpster?" Jess asked.

"Hell yes, I did," he said. "She would smother me in my sleep if I spent more than fifty bucks on a Christmas gift. Her favorite thing about the damn purse is it was free."

"With time being a factor," Scott interjected, "I say we focus on the dumpsters at a college. It's mid-May, so the kids are moving off campus."

"Oh, he's right." Anthony nodded. "Excellent strategy."

"Tactics are kind of my thing," Scott said.

"Sorry," Lauren said. "Did you say *we*?"

Scott looked at Ivy and said, "Yeah, we." He patted Brenner on the shoulder and said, "We're going to assist with the dumpster diving."

Brenner was caught off guard a bit, but not at all surprised Scott would volunteer their services to two women determined to sort through trash late at night.

"If you don't want us to tag along, we'll stay right here and watch the app for updates." Scott put his hands in his pockets and said, "I think it will be tons of fun finding you something to photograph for this contest. I want to help you win."

"Thank you," said Lauren. "But I don't want to interrupt your…" she looked at Brenner, "reunion, maybe? You both were having a great time catching up before I…"

Brenner enjoyed the blush on Lauren's cheeks but didn't like knowing she was still embarrassed. "We were done gabbing, anyway," he said. "If you let us help, you'll get to the next challenge faster."

"I'd take them up on the offer," Jess said. "You could do so much worse than having two handsome war heroes watch your back."

Ivy raised one eyebrow. "War heroes?"

"Ah," said Scott. "You know how Jess exaggerates."

"I never, ever exaggerate," Jess said. "Sully is a true American hero. As a matter of fact, he—"

"Hey, we don't have time for boring war stories," Scott said, talking over Jess. His voice during the interruption was a mixture of lightheartedness and modesty. His eyes, however, pleaded for discretion and privacy.

Brenner redirected the conversation back to Lauren. "Time is ticking, right?"

"Right," Lauren said. "So we should try a college first?"

"Oh yeah," said Scott. "College kids are too lazy to resist a dumpster when moving off campus."

"If nothing else, you'll score a few hundred bucks worth of textbooks you can sell on Amazon," said Dave. "At best, you'll find furniture, clothes, art, or other stuff students can't fit in a tiny Prius."

"How about Regents College?" Lauren suggested. "We can park near the corner of Queens and Wesley?"

"Sounds good," said Brenner. "We'll meet you there."

Scott pulled his phone out of his pocket as he walked over to Ivy. "Listen, I was going to ask if I could get your number for personal reasons," he said with a wink. Then he changed his posture and stood at attention. "But since we're now allies on a covert mission, I do need your number." He offered her his phone.

"Why?" she asked as she took it from him.

"Confirming tactics and OPSEC."

"Oh right, tactics and OPSEC...for the mission," Ivy said. Scott smiled as she entered her information.

She called her number with his phone and when her

purse started ringing, she said, "I would have given you my number anyway."

"That's the best news I've heard in a long while, Ivy," he said. "Let's see your screen and confirm it wasn't a coincidence."

Ivy rolled her eyes. "You watched me call my own phone." She lifted her phone out of the side pocket of her purse and flashed the screen in Scott's direction. "See?"

Scott squinted at the phone before backing up a step. "Who's Mark?"

Everyone at Jess's and Margot's tables gasped. "Oh! It gets better and better!" said Margot. Raising her empty mason jar in the air, she said, "Another round, Sir Anthony!"

Jess turned in her chair to face Margot. "How many have you had?"

She looked at her friends, shrugged and said, "A couple."

"Two of those drinks is more than enough. You need a round of waters. Now, shhh!" Jess said as she turned back to watch Scott and Ivy and her cell phone.

After Scott's reaction, Ivy turned her phone around to see the screen. Ivy's face was just as surprised.

"What's wrong?" asked Lauren.

"Mark texted to confirm we're meeting at midnight."

Scott looked Ivy in the eyes. "Is Mark your boyfriend?"

"No. I don't have a boyfriend. But, I do have plans with Mark," she said. "It's a second date."

"What kind of second date starts at midnight?" Scott stood up straight and put his hands on his hips.

Ivy copied the posture and hand placement. "We're seeing Scott Eastwood's new movie." When Scott didn't respond, she said, "He plays a Delta Force recruit who gets separated from his unit during training and has to save the President by himself."

"Cool. I love fairy tales." Scott rolled his eyes, and Brenner coughed into his fist. "But why go to the midnight showing?"

"I'm moderately obsessed with Scott Eastwood." Ivy shrugged one shoulder, and Lauren laughed. "Okay, so my obsession could be classified as moderate to severe," Ivy amended. "It's something you should know about me. I make no apologies."

"I got no problem with you crushing on some actor who's been in like three movies—"

"Twenty-six," Ivy interrupted.

Scott waved his hand and kept speaking, "—but hearing you're going on a second date with Mark is about to ruin the best night I've had in a long while."

"I'm more excited about watching the movie than seeing Mark." Ivy's thumbs flew over the bottom half of her phone. "What's your last name?" she asked with her thumbs frozen over the keyboard at the bottom of the screen.

"Sullivan." He watched her type his name and add him to her contacts.

"Ah. Now, 'Sully' makes sense. Should I call you 'Sully' too?"

"I'd rather you didn't. My friends call me 'Sully,' and I don't want to be your friend."

Ivy laughed. "You don't want to be my friend?"

"Nope." Scott shook his head and smiled. "Please cancel your plans with Mark."

"I'll consider it." Ivy slid her phone into her purse.

"You promise to take me to see the movie tomorrow?"

"Gal Gadot is in the movie too, so hell yes. It's a win-win." Scott took a deep breath before he continued. "Our date will be the first of many."

"Oh, you think so?"

"I know so, and I'd like to go on record as stating hashtag number six is going to be epic."

CHAPTER FIVE

Lauren

"I'M SORRY TO INTERRUPT," LAUREN SAID, "but if I drop to tenth place before we leave this bar, I will lose my shit." She was only half joking. "Y'all can iron out your movie date later."

"She's right, you two." Brenner walked over and stood between Scott and Ivy. "We need to hustle."

Ivy jumped a bit and said, "Right! Let's go." She abruptly left where she was standing and positioned herself next to Lauren. She looked her friend in the eyes and mouthed, "I am so sorry."

Lauren's impatience with Ivy faded fast. "He's a handsome war hero named Scott of all things." She lightheartedly rolled her eyes at Ivy and said, "You can make up for any delays with your mad torch app skills."

"You can count on it." Ivy's shoulders sagged in relief. "Thank you for understanding."

Lauren looked at the people still gathered around the tables. "Anthony. Dave. Thank you for your helpful suggestions."

Dave tipped his longneck beer bottle toward Lauren

and said, "Happy hunting!"

Anthony showed Lauren his phone and said, "I'll be watching the app for updates. Good luck!"

Addressing Margot's table, Lauren said, "You ladies are awesome. Be safe tonight and promise me you'll Uber home."

"Promise!" Margot yelled from her table. "But let's get a quick picture before you go!"

It was the last thing Lauren wanted to do, but after taking a deep breath, she nodded and said, "Sure thing."

"Once you win," Margot said, "we can prove we were here for the 'find a hottie' and 'dive in a dumpster' parts of your contest."

"I'll grab the camera," said Jess. She ran behind the bar as Lauren, Ivy, Brenner, Scott, Anthony, Dave, Margot and the others assembled themselves as best they could around the table.

Jess held a vintage Polaroid instant camera up to her eye and shouted, "Alright, everybody… Say 'Barkley's!'"

"BARKLEY'S!"

After the film was ejected from the camera, a round of hugs, high fives, and well wishes ensued among the people who had posed for the picture. Lauren and Ivy found Jess shaking the film dry. "Sorry about all the chaos tonight."

"I'm starting to worry this is the calm before the storm." She pointed a pinkie to Margot who was taking selfies with Anthony, shouting, "Hashtag hotties!" Jess shook her head. "I promised them another round, but I'm hoping the moonshine has already affected their short-term memory." Jess handed Lauren the picture. "It's almost dry. I'll be right back."

While Jess grabbed the stapler by the bar's register,

Lauren watched the image streak to life. Once the image was fully developed, she was grateful Margot had insisted on capturing this moment. Lauren took a picture of it with her phone and posted it on Instagram with a quick caption: #GroupShot @BarkleysPub while on #TheHashtagHunt. When Jess returned, she took the Polaroid from Lauren and stapled it on the wall next to the others.

"I still need to settle up our tab," Lauren said. She slipped her credit card out of the wallet case on her cell phone and offered it to Jess.

Jess shook her head at Lauren and then looked at the picture. "This," she said, pointing to Scott's wide smile, "is why your tab is on me tonight. Sully deserves more smiles like this one after all he's been through." Turning her attention to Ivy, she said, "If you make this smile disappear, it will be my mission to make you regret it."

"Listen, Jess, his smile is my new favorite thing," Ivy said, studying the picture. "I will do my best to keep it there."

To Lauren, Jess said, "Good luck with the rest of the pictures, girl." She tapped the edge of the Polaroid twice. "We're all rooting for you."

"Thanks, Jess." With a final wave to the people in the bar, Lauren and Ivy joined Brenner and Scott.

"Ready to dive in some dumpsters?" Lauren asked.

"We were born ready," Scott said. He ran ahead to open the door, but reached it so quickly, Ivy and Lauren were shocked still. "After you," he said as he opened the door. Scott flicked his eyes to Brenner. "Last chance to go home to your rom-coms and kitten jammies."

Noticing Ivy and Lauren were not walking toward the open door, Scott said, "I thought we were hustling here."

"Thank you," Lauren said as she followed Ivy to the door.

"You bet."

Lauren could have sworn Scott exhibited some type of super speed, but she dismissed the thought as ludicrous. Since the moment she got the first text from the Wizard, she'd been wound tight and out of sorts.

Ivy must have seen it too, however, because she stopped in front of Scott at the door. "You were…really fast… Like lightning fast."

With a wink, he said, "Only when I want to be."

Lauren followed Ivy out the door and whispered in her ear, "'Only when I want to be.' That was smooth."

"Yes," Ivy whispered back. "Momma like."

Once the men had joined them outside, Ivy said in a normal volume, "Oh look, Lauren!" She pointed to one of the vehicles in the parking lot and said, "Too bad the Wizard didn't make 'Lauren's kryptonite' the next hashtag."

"You like trucks, Lauren?" Scott asked with a smile.

She admired the pristine, blacked-out pickup with running boards and tinted windows. "I do when they look like this." She pointed to the truck. "Doesn't even matter if it's a Ford, Chevy, Dodge—"

"Okay, now you're blasphemous."

"I'm serious. Any big, black truck will do," Lauren said with a laugh. "I think it's the native Texan in me, but they always turn my head."

"You don't say," Scott said as they all walked behind the truck. "How interesting."

"Why?" Ivy asked. "Is the truck yours?"

"Sorry to disappoint, but no. I'm more of a classic muscle car kind of guy. This is me," he said, walking up to a 1968 powder blue Ford Mustang. He pulled his keys out of his pocket, but turned toward Brenner, "Hey, do you mind driving, B?" Running his hand over the hood, he said, "I was reunited with my baby earlier today, and I'd rather not take her dumpster diving." He returned the keys to his pocket. "Your ride could come in handy tonight. No telling what we'll find over at Regents. I might score a new sofa."

Brenner rolled his eyes and started walking in the direction they had come from. Once he pressed a button on his key fob, the taillights on the big, black truck flashed.

Scott laughed. "Let's get the gear sorted before we leave," he said. "No telling what kind of light we'll have around the dumpsters."

Brenner opened his door and pulled a rucksack from behind the driver's seat. He pitched it to Scott with more force than necessary and smiled when his friend let out an aggravated "Umph."

To Lauren, Brenner said, "I'd hoped he would be cool about the truck conversation, but I clearly underestimated his willingness to embarrass me whenever possible."

"Embarrass *you*?" she said. "I actually thought I might get past the whole 'I was busted taking your picture because you're hot' situation in the bar. I thought I might be able to look you in the eye sometime."

In a low voice, he said, "You have incredibly beautiful eyes, Lauren. I'd like to see more of them, not less. Please don't let Scott ruin it for me."

Lauren blushed as her gaze moved from Brenner to her shoes, then across the asphalt to watch Scott and Ivy poke through the contents of Brenner's backpack. After retrieving a headlamp and a flashlight for Ivy, Scott closed the ruck and tossed it on the passenger seat.

"Time to go, kids!" Scott said with a smirk. Ivy carried the borrowed gear to Lauren's car.

Brenner turned to Lauren. "I'll follow you to Regents."

"Sounds good." Lauren pulled her key fob from her front pocket and walked toward her car. After the beep and the click of the doors unlocking, Lauren opened her car door and sat behind the wheel. As soon as Ivy shut her door on the passenger side, she turned to Lauren and said, "I am so sorry about the kryptonite comment. I had no idea it was his truck."

"Oh, I know it wasn't on purpose. It's okay." Lauren tossed the key fob in a cupholder and plugged her cell phone into the car charger. After pushing the ignition button, she sank into the seat and said, "I keep embarrassing myself around him...in huge, epic ways. I must come across as a shallow, superficial idiot."

"Not true." Ignoring the look Lauren was giving her, Ivy lowered the visor above her to check her makeup. "For what it's worth, I think Brenner was flattered." Satisfied with her reflection, she raised the visor with a finger. "You think he's hot. You love his truck."

Lauren laughed as she fastened her seat belt. "I also love whiskey and America, so basically, I'm a country song." Lauren reversed from her spot and drove out of the parking lot.

Ivy was laughing too. "Well, it could be worse." She pulled her phone out of her purse and waved it side to side. "You could be about to break a smoking hot date with a sweaty Scott Eastwood dressed in camo."

"I get you're attracted to Scott." Lauren jerked her thumb above her right shoulder. "I mean that Scott. Although, I am surprised you're missing the movie because of a guy you just met." She looked in her rearview mirror and admired the sleek truck following her car. She knew she wasn't a shallow person, but she couldn't help it. Some women liked shoes, she liked trucks.

"Um, yeah. It's unlike me, but this one's a no-brainer." Out of the corner of her eye, Lauren saw Ivy scrolling through her contacts. "If I'm honest, I was dreading the date with Mark, and I can't wait to spend more time with Scott again."

"You're going to see Scott again in like seven minutes."

"I know!" Ivy wiggled in her seat. "Let me call Mark real fast."

"Not texting him?"

"This is more than canceling our date tonight. I don't want to make any future plans with the guy, so this conversation deserves a phone call."

Lauren lifted her hand for a high five, and Ivy gave her one.

"Honesty saves everyone's time. I've had enough guys ghost on me or spoon feed me lies," Ivy said.

"Like the guy who said he was in bed with the flu and then got tagged in a Facebook photo an hour later?"

"Yes, exactly like that jackass." Ivy tapped on her phone's screen. "What an idiot. I mean, grow a pair already and—Oh, hey, Mark! Huh? No, I wasn't talking to you, I swear." Ivy laughed, and Lauren could hear the relief in Mark's voice through the phone. "I was venting about someone else when you picked up."

Ivy looked out the passenger side window and sighed. "The reason for my call is to tell you I'm not going to make the movie." She fidgeted with the hemline of her dress. "Um, a couple of reasons. The biggest one is my best friend, Lauren, is in a photo contest. I caught up with her after work and helped with the last two challenges. She's in second place!" Ivy turned her head to wink at Lauren. "I know, it's great. She still has a way to go, so I'm going to keep helping."

Lauren blew Ivy a kiss. She didn't know where she'd be without Ivy's help. While she'd never borrow a dime of Ivy's inheritance, she cherished having her friend by her side tonight. They'd been ride or die since college. She wasn't trying to eavesdrop, but she couldn't help but hear Mark suggest seeing the movie another day.

Ivy took a deep breath. "Another reason I am calling to cancel our date… I respect you, so I want to be straightforward here. Despite having a nice time last week, I don't see this going anywhere."

Lauren could not make out what Mark was saying, but she respected the even tone of his voice.

"Well, thank you," Ivy said. "I appreciate it. I wish you the best of luck, Mark. Bye." Ivy ended her call. "Now, let's get down to business. I'll search for 'dumpster diving on a college campus.'"

"Just like that?" Lauren looked over and saw Ivy scrolling through the search results.

"Huh?" Ivy looked up from her phone. "Just like what?"

"Switching gears to Google after breaking Mark's heart?"

"Oh, he'll be fine," Ivy said with a dismissive wave. "Like they say, 'A clear rejection is always better than a fake promise.'"

"Who says that?"

"Pinterest, baby," Ivy said, still scrolling. "My life-quotes board is my digital Dalai Lama."

Lauren laughed and said, "Well, I agree with whatever meme you're channeling here. You did the right thing."

"It's best to be honest." Ivy paused her scrolling to say, "And tonight with the man bun, the bar, the handsome heroes, Margot…" She looked out the windshield and smiled. Lauren assumed Ivy was thinking about Scott and was surprised when Ivy said, "I actually went an hour or so without thinking about my dad."

Lauren's heart ached for her friend. She'd been jealous of the close relationship Ivy had had with her father, and she knew she'd never grasp the depth of Ivy's grief. "Maybe it's a good thing to give your heart and mind something else to think about for a while."

"It is a great thing." Ivy took a deep breath. "You may need the cash, but I need the contest, my friend."

"Even if it includes dumpsters?" Lauren said in mock panic.

"Even if, but full disclosure: I'm officially dreading hashtags seven through twelve."

"Me too." Lauren had been thinking the same thing. "Maybe the Wizard is weeding out the people not committed to the contest. See if they'll quit when things get hard."

"Or illegal. And I wouldn't blame them for quitting." Ivy shifted in the passenger seat to look out the back window. "Good thing we have backup. Those two handsome veterans are going to make this hashtag happen." She faced forward and said, "You are so going to win the money. I know it."

"Hey, back at the bar, when you and Jess were discussing Scott's smile in the Polaroid picture…" Lauren glanced to her right, and Ivy nodded. "It's great to see you smiling again. You've been through a lot too."

"Yeah, most days I fake it until I get home, but tonight I didn't force myself to smile once," Ivy said as they arrived at the campus. "The man bun and the hottie were fun. Supporting you and Paperback Vinyl is fun. Flirting with Scott is fun."

"Pretty sure he thinks you're fun," Lauren said as she pulled into a visitors' parking lot. "But I need this photo, so pause for my cause." She winked at Ivy. "You can flirt all you want after the dumpster dive."

"You promise?"

"I do."

CHAPTER SIX

Brenner

ON THE WAY TO REGENTS COLLEGE, BRENNER TEASED SCOTT about his Flash impersonation at the bar. Scott's response was an explanation of the innovative bionics, giving Brenner a crash course in cybernetics and complex polymers. Brenner didn't follow how Scott's brain controlled the robotics, but he grasped the significance of the advancements. Scott's positive attitude about his "new normal" was more impressive than the prosthetic legs. Brenner doubted he'd be as composed as Sully in similar circumstances. He may have returned with all his body parts, but he'd lost his peace of mind.

"All right, Super Soldier, close it up," Brenner said as they followed Lauren's car into the visitors' parking lot.

Scott closed the battery compartment and tugged down the hem of his jeans. "Do me a solid: when we're around the ladies, act like I have boring, human legs."

"Do *you* a solid?" Brenner pulled in a parking spot and shoved the gear shift to Park. "After the stunt you pulled with my truck?"

"Now hold on." Scott unfastened his seat belt. "You

own the truck she admired. It would've come out eventually…maybe. Probably." He shrugged before opening the passenger door. "And for what it's worth, 'Kryptonite' would've made a killer call sign." Scott got out of the truck and closed the door.

Brenner watched his friend walk away, thankfully at a respectable pace this time. After grabbing his rucksack, he locked the truck and joined the others on the sidewalk. Scott and Ivy watched him approach, but Lauren's attention never left her phone's screen. Brenner could understand if she was using the device to avoid eye contact. Her embarrassment from explaining "hottie in the wild" had only intensified after Ivy's "kryptonite" comment. He'd been flattered on both counts, but he empathized and hoped Lauren's discomfort would lessen. He'd bonded with strangers at boot camp, and Brenner was confident dumpster diving would break the ice.

"Alright," Scott said with a clap. "We'll head north until we hit the senior dorm. Behind the building, a walkway curves to the right and leads to the dumpster."

Ivy couldn't contain her surprise. "How do you know where the dumpster is?"

"My CO owed me a favor, so I called him on the drive over. He sent the latest satellite imagery of this area over a secure line."

"You're kidding," said Lauren.

"Yeah, I'm kidding." Scott pulled out his phone. "I looked up Regents on Google Earth and made a screenshot." He showed them the photo. "I zoomed in on what must be a dorm, and here," he said, pointing to a hazy brown and blue rectangle on the screen, "is a dumpster. Or at least it looks like one from this view."

"Impressive." Ivy rolled her eyes. "And here we were planning on walking around the campus until we found a dorm with a dumpster."

"Civilians." Scott looked at Brenner and laughed.

They started down the sidewalk, and after a few steps, Scott reached out and took hold of Ivy's hand. She gave him an odd look. "Safety first, Miss Ivy," he said. "Don't want you to trip and fall for someone else on the way."

Ivy groaned and said, "Worst line ever."

Lifting their joined fingers, Scott said, "Yet it worked. And trust me, I can do much worse when it comes to lame pickup lines." After a few moments, he asked, "Do people hold hands anymore? Should we Snapchat a two-person filter while we're walking side by side? Or we could take a selfie and post it on the Gram? Tag you and make it my profile pic?"

Ivy laughed. "Well," she lifted their hands as he had. "This works. If you're holding my hand instead of your phone, I feel like I have your attention."

"Do. You. Ever." Scott brought her hand to his lips and kissed the area near her wrist. "I should play it cool and act like meeting you isn't a big deal, but life has taught me absolutely anything can disappear in the blink of an eye. So while you're right here, I need to tell you: meeting you is a big deal. Huge, in fact."

"We've known each other for five minutes, Scott. You don't know me."

"Life has also taught me how to read people. I could tell right away that you're a selfless person and a great friend to Lauren. You've got a kind soul and a fierce spirit... and a beautiful heart," Scott said. "And if you don't mind me saying, it's all wrapped up in one gorgeous package,

Sweets. You're beautiful inside and out, which is a quality everyone finds irresistible."

Ivy shook her head. "Bet you say that to all the girls."

"I've never said those words to anyone before right now." Scott squeezed her hand. "And yes…it's been five minutes, but they've been some of the best of my life. I'd like more time to get to know you."

Brenner and Lauren were walking a few paces behind them and overheard their friends' conversation. "I'm sure you didn't expect to chaperone those two in the middle of your contest," Brenner said. When Lauren looked up from her phone, he gestured toward the couple ahead of them on the sidewalk. "I hope their stolen moments at the bar didn't cost you the prize money."

"I've been checking the app." Lauren smiled and tilted her phone to the left so Brenner could see the screen. "I'm still in second place."

"That's a relief." Brenner's gaze went from the screen to Lauren's eyes. The sound of laughter made Brenner and Lauren look away from each other and toward Ivy and Scott. "Thanks again for letting us crash your contest. We love a good mission…and Scott wasn't ready to say good-bye to Ivy."

"I'd say the feeling's mutual." Lauren smiled and slid her phone into her back pocket. "And if Ivy's happy, I'm happy. He seems like a great guy."

"Sully's the best." Brenner cleared his throat before saying, "So, when the contest is over, maybe we—"

"This is it." Scott looked over his shoulder, apparently unaware of his interruption. "Wallace Belk Senior Residence Hall." He pointed to a poster on the bulletin board next to the double door. *Graduates! Caps & Gowns are in Room 112*. Beneath the announcement, "Bye, Felicia!" was scribbled in Sharpie.

Brenner's focus went from the bulletin board to the entrance of the three-story dormitory. The classical portico was well lit and had discreet surveillance equipment installed above the heavy wooden doors. Brenner was all for campus security, but for Lauren's sake, he hoped it was less considerable at the dumpster area.

As usual, Scott voiced what Brenner was thinking. "We'll employ strict noise and light discipline."

Ivy squinted at Scott. "We'll do what?"

"I doubt security at the dumpster is this tight, but let's avoid attention until we know the conditions."

Brenner scanned the area for students. "It's Friday night. Where is everyone?"

"My guess is they're studying hard or partying harder. Some may have already moved out and left us some goodies behind," Scott said. "Let's go find out." He raised a finger to his lips, and Ivy, Lauren, and Brenner nodded.

They followed the sidewalk as it wrapped around the dorm, halting when Scott triggered a motion-sensor light installed on the upper corner of the building. The street was illuminated, but the pathway to the dumpster extended beyond the beam of light. Scott pointed down the path and then moved his hand back and forth repeatedly near the center of his forehead in a karate-chopping motion.

Lauren tilted her head and creased her forehead in confusion. Ivy shrugged her shoulders and copied his hand movement until she smacked the side of her pointer finger on her forehead. Brenner huffed a quiet laugh and waved at the women to get their attention. He used his right hand to show walking fingers and mouthed, "Single file." Ivy rolled her eyes and gave Scott an exaggerated two thumbs up. Brenner edged around them and continued past the dorm. Lauren followed, and Ivy and Scott fell in line behind them.

As predicted, the path curved to the right, leading them away from the dorm and other common areas. Brenner was grateful the college was concerned with aesthetics because the discreet dumpster location served their mission well. As he drew near the enclosure, a lamppost came into view, casting a soft glow on the end of the path. The black resin pole was topped with a glass globe and black finial. The decorative fixture matched the ones he'd noticed scattered across campus. Brenner smiled because they cast a soft glow, much dimmer than the LED fixtures on the dorm and in the parking lot. He'd seen a report about historical universities retrofitting antique fixtures with brighter bulbs to improve campus security. Many schools were fundraising for the expensive LED modifications, but Regents College hadn't yet converted their lampposts. Brenner was relieved because the dumpster was not as well lit as it could have been.

The front gate was propped open by a broken futon. When they had all reached the end of the path, Lauren whispered, "If the door's wide open, we're not breaking in, right?"

Scott nodded and said, "I doubt we'll run into any trouble this time of night."

Brenner scanned the area again to confirm no others were nearby. "All clear." He took a few steps into the enclosure and was surprised to see the dumpster took up half the space. To the left was an assortment of items left for bulky-waste collection. He waved the others into the area and pointed to the pile. In a soft voice, he said, "Let's look here first." It did not take long to dismiss each item near the bin, including a folding table with three legs, a filthy box fan, an artificial Christmas tree missing several branches, and a fifty-inch TV with a shattered flat screen. Even the unbroken items were not contenders for the contest.

"Well, that would have been too easy, I guess," said Lauren.

Brenner looked over the bulky items, searching for something sturdy enough to hold his weight. He chose a discarded mini fridge and large storage tub with rope handles. He shoved the refrigerator against the dumpster and placed the tub upside down next to it. "The good stuff must be in the trash. Let's go find it." He pulled his gloves and flashlight out of his rucksack before nimbly stepping on top of the fridge. He raised the rigid plastic cover off the dumpster, setting it back on its hinges so it would stay open. Then Brenner turned, bent down, and offered a hand to Lauren.

Lauren stared at his hand a moment before taking it and stepping onto the round base of the tub. "This is happening, isn't it?" she murmured. They stood close beside each other, both looking into the dumpster.

Brenner handed Lauren his flashlight and pointed to the opposite side of the dumpster. "Aim the light over there." When the area was illuminated, he swung one leg into the bin and placed his boot on a metal gusset attached to the inside corner. With one gloved hand on the frame for balance, he moved his other leg inside and sat on the narrow edge of the metal wall. He pointed to Scott waiting below and said, "You're up."

Scott set the headlamp over Ivy's hair, adjusting the straps so it would fit her forehead. He held her head in his hands and rubbed his thumbs against her cheeks twice. "When we're done here, I might smell like hot trash." He stepped back and put his gloves on. "Please don't hold it against me."

"If you do, it's because you helped Lauren not smell like hot trash." Ivy smiled. "I can live with that."

Scott used the mini fridge to reach the top of the dumpster and joined Brenner on the edge, facing the trash. Lauren helped Ivy step up onto the refrigerator and then returned the flashlight's beam to the area Brenner had indicated. Ivy turned on her headlamp and angled it to the other half of the dumpster.

"The first one to find something awesome wins," said Scott. He used his arms for balance as he scooted down the ledge.

Brenner made his way to the opposite corner. "Deal."

"Wins what?" Ivy adjusted the headlamp. "Tetanus?"

Scott laughed before he answered. "Winner buys a shirt the loser must wear in public. Hey, B, you still have the *My Little Pony* shirt?"

"I was saving it for when I win fantasy football, but the purple glitter got everywhere. It had to go." Brenner lowered himself into the dumpster and balanced on a narrow support beam. He began shifting trash bags around, looking for large, random items under the surface.

Lauren asked, "Is it too late for you to sign a waiver?"

With a smile, Brenner said, "It's actually not bad in here. Sully and I have stood in much worse."

Scott reached down into the trash and tugged something toward him. "What could this be?" It took him both hands to lift an egg crate crammed with trophies and awards. When he set it down on a pile of trash to his right, the pile compacted under the weight. Once the trash stopped moving, he removed a trophy from the crate. "Ivy, aim your headlamp over here a minute." He removed a trophy and held it up to the light. The column was made out of plastic tubing painted to look like a marble pillar. A green four-leaf clover sat on top, wrapped in a "Better Luck Next Time" banner. Scott read the inscription out loud: "'Participation Award. Greek Olympics - You Were There.'"

"Harsh." Ivy pointed to the crate. "I'd throw it away too."

"Agreed." Scott tossed the trophy into the trash beside him. "Let's see if they're all from frat boys." He lifted a heavy award shaped like a hot-water bottle. "'Douchebag of the Year.' Did the campus bullies have a banquet?" He dropped the award into the trash. "Shame, I thought this crap had potential." He lifted the rest up one at a time, reading the plaques to himself before tossing them deeper into the dumpster. "Okay, this one is funny." It was a trophy made from an AXE body spray can. "'It's Basically a Shower, Bro.'"

Brenner laughed and returned his attention to the area around him. "We should make one for Murray. He loves him some AXE body spray."

"He's the only one who does." Scott waded to his left. "You know it's a problem when an entire battalion returning from drill smells better than Murray headed out on date night."

"True story." Brenner laughed and moved a few more trash bags from the area near his knees. He bent down and tugged on a curved piece of cardboard. It was a life-size cutout folded in thirds. "Let's see who we got." He unfolded the creases and revealed a half-naked Channing Tatum.

"Magic Mike!" Lauren pointed out the deterioration around the actor's mouth, hands, torso, and groin. "Oh, what did they do to you?"

"Nothing good." Brenner refolded the cardboard cutout and shoved it deep in the dumpster. Then he found a box in decent shape with handwriting on the side. He used his pocket flashlight to illuminate the words scrawled in bold black marker. "Okay. This could be promising." He lifted the box and placed it on the ledge next to him. Lauren's flashlight allowed everyone to read the writing: *Broken Dreams and Failures*.

Scott walked toward Brenner and made it look easy, despite wading through boxes and trash bags. Brenner wondered if having perfect balance or an auto-leveling feature was another bionic perk. Scott sliced through the packing tape with his penknife. Brenner noticed similar boxes near his feet and bent down to read the writing. "If box number one is a bust, we can open *Zombie Defense System* and *Taxidermy School Projects*."

"Oh yay. Somebody's got jokes." Ivy shook her head, making the light from her headlamp jerk left to right. "This whole scene is nasty enough without bringing taxidermy into the mix."

"Keep the light steady and aim it here," Scott said, tapping the top of the *Broken Dreams and Failures* box. Once it was well lit, he opened the box and revealed shiny hardback book covers. "Maybe there's a gem in here." Scott lifted the box and waded through the trash toward Lauren.

"We could sell them on Amazon," said Lauren. "Or maybe there isn't much demand for these books," she amended, reading the titles as she lifted them from the box.

"*Microsoft Access*…with CD-ROM, *Introduction to Darkroom Developing, Calculus of a Single Variable.*"

"Ugh," said Ivy, looking into the box. "Is it all so boring?"

"I hope not. Here, hold these." Lauren passed the top three books to Ivy and continued to look through the box.

Ivy set the software and calculus textbooks down by her feet. She held up the darkroom textbook and pointed to the old enlarger on the cover. "My uncle has one of these in his basement. He wants a darkroom…" She flipped through the pages and said, "He thinks film is making a comeback."

"He's right," Brenner said as he waded through the dumpster. "There was an article in *Time* magazine a while ago about photographers returning to the lost art of film."

"Why would they do that?" Scott asked.

"To stand out. With apps and filters, anybody with a phone can create a cool image, but it takes serious skill and patience to capture something great on film." Brenner noticed something smooth and white near his knee and he bent to investigate it further. "Hey, Lauren, what do you think about this?" He lifted a bowling pin by the neck. It had been repurposed into a lamp and included a brass socket for a bulb and a knotted power cord dangling from the base.

"You've got to be kidding!" Scott looked from the bowling pin to Lauren and back again. "It's a lamp? Someone threw that away?"

Ivy leveled a stare at Brenner. "What have you done?"

"I should have known it would catch his eye. My apologies." Brenner tossed the bowling pin to Scott.

"How about this for your treasure trash photo?" Scott

presented the lamp to Lauren.

"Um...it's a contender." Lauren smiled at Ivy's grimace. "We'll hang on to it in case it's the best we find."

"Oh, I'm hanging on to it. Finders. Keepers." Scott looked down at the bowling pin and whistled before jerking his head back up. In a strained voice, he said, "Unless one of you wanted it." After Ivy, Lauren, and Brenner declined interest in owning the lamp, Scott said, "Well, then this bad boy is coming home with me. NOICE!"

Ivy wrinkled her nose and said, "Are you for real right now?"

Lauren put her hand on Ivy's shoulder and said, "You can debate home decor tomorrow." She looked at Scott. "You think it's a good dumpster dive find? Good enough to enter?"

"Hell yes!" Scott looked it over for a moment before jerking his head up with an incredulous expression. "What's not to like?"

Ivy said, "How much time you got?"

"Oh, spare me." Scott lifted the lamp and said, "Spare me...get it? He carried the bowling pin lamp to where Ivy was standing. "Set this down for me? Please."

"Man, it's a good thing you're cute." Ivy balanced the darkroom textbook on the ledge of the dumpster and took the lamp from Scott. She held it far from her body as she lowered it to the ground. "You'll scrub and disinfect it, right? Multiple times?"

"Are you a germaphobe, Sweets?" Scott asked.

"I am around dumpsters," she said. "And porta-potties, ATMs, and gas pumps."

"You know, sometimes bacteria are the only culture people have."

"Enough with the dad jokes, old man."

Scott pointed to the black scuffs streaked on the head of the pin. "These are from its glory days knocking around a bowling alley. I can replace the wiring if it's shot." Scott looked at Ivy. "So, on our second date, let's find a lamp-shade worthy of—"

"Our second date?"

"Yes, ma'am."

"One date could be plenty."

"Impossible. I know I'll want more time with you. I already do."

CHAPTER SEVEN

Lauren

"**F**OCUS, MAN." LAUREN DUCKED AS SOMETHING RED HIT and bounced off Scott's back. "No more date discussions until the contest's over."

"Dumpster trash, B? Really?" Scott looked behind him and picked up the red plastic flowerpot Brenner had thrown. In the center was a "Hello, my name is" name tag, and Scott lifted the planter to read the name handwritten in the blank space. "'Robert Plant.'" After a beat of silence, laughter rose up from the enclosure.

"That's great," said Lauren.

"I wonder if they tossed the plant out too?" Brenner looked around the area where he'd found the container. "We could put him back together for a photo."

Scott nodded. "Robert Plant would make a great dumpster dive find."

"I'll hang on to the flowerpot in case the plant's down there too." Lauren took the planter from Scott and set it down next to the bowling pin. "Okay, so we have half of a lamp and half of a well-named dorm plant."

"It's a decent start." Ivy picked up the darkroom

textbook. "I know this goes against what I said earlier, but I might give this book to my uncle. It's in excellent condition."

Scott laughed. "Someone's catching on."

Ivy ran her fingers over the glossy hardcover. "It was sealed shut in a box, not decaying in the corner of the dumpster." She flipped through the pages and discovered a piece of paper wedged between the last few pages of the book. Ivy tugged the paper free from the crease and said, "What have we here?" She unfolded the paper, skimmed over the first few lines, and read it aloud.

T-

Julie and I ate at Trios tonight, and next to our table was a cute couple stammering their way through their first date. He was nervous, and she was shy. It was equal parts awkward and adorable, and I was inspired to write this letter…for a few reasons:

In Case You Didn't Know - I doubt I'll ever stop falling in love with you. As soon as I think I can't possibly love you more, you do something wonderful. Like when you sent flowers to my grandma on her birthday. Or flew home to console me when Rascal had to be put down. Or had a heart-shaped pizza and red wine delivered on the only Valentine's Day we didn't spend together. I love your "Good Morning" texts, silly pictures, and all the ways you confirm I'm on your mind and in your heart. So many of my smiles are because of you.

Gentle Reminder - This long-distance situation is far from ideal, and I miss you terribly. I'm a little jealous of the people who get to see you every day, but I know this last semester has a shelf life. The miles between us are hard to bear but much more comfortable to take than a life without you. In time, we'll be together in the same state, city, neighborhood, home, bed. Anticipating your next visit makes me smile…and blush a little.

Confession - I almost bailed on our first date. I didn't know what to wear or what to eat. I didn't know what to say and wondered what we'd have in common. I had dozens of what-if scenarios, and I was every bit as nervous as the couple on their first date tonight. Hindsight shows me I should've never doubted us then, which makes it easy to never question us now. Each day that passes brings us closer, in all the ways that count.

I love you, and I love being yours. Thank you for making me ridiculously happy.

- M

"This is a legit love letter!" Ivy turned and handed the stationery to Lauren. "It's one thousand percent the nicest thing we'll find in this dumpster."

Lauren read the letter silently and then looked around the piles of discarded items. "This is better than half a lamp and an empty flowerpot. You think the Wizard will like it?"

"She'll love it."

"The Wizard's a she?" Brenner asked. When Lauren and Ivy nodded, he said, "I agree with Ivy. A handwritten love letter is a rare item. I know it will get you to the next hashtag."

Lauren opened her phone's camera with one hand and raised the letter with the other. The dumpster's contents were visible behind the paper, and she liked the contrast between black plastic bags, crumpled beige cardboard, powder blue stationery, and navy blue ink. Once the handwriting was in focus, Lauren took the picture and studied the composition. She was about to take a second photo when she heard feminine voices beyond the dumpster enclosure.

Ivy aimed her headlamp toward the noise, shining the

bright light on two young women entering the area.

"Ah! I'm blind!" One woman listed to the left and stumbled into the barren Christmas tree. She dropped the clear plastic bin she'd been holding and clung to the tree's remaining branches. "What the hell?"

The other woman was right on her heels. "Easy there, killer." She helped her friend let go of the tree and shielded her eyes when she turned to Ivy. "Can you turn off the spotlight?"

"Sorry!" Ivy turned the headlamp off and removed it from her forehead. "You ladies okay?"

"Never better," said the first woman. With glassy eyes and staggered steps, she drew closer to the dumpster. Her gaze panned from Brenner and Scott knee-deep in the trash to Ivy and Lauren standing on top of bulky items shoved against the dumpster. Clearly intoxicated, she shook her head and said, "We won't be here long."

Her friend picked up the bin from the ground and said, "I got this."

Lauren still hadn't sent the picture of the love letter to the Wizard. She tried to make out what was in the clear plastic bin, but it was difficult from where she stood. "If you don't mind me asking, are you about to throw away anything valuable?"

"Hell no. It's all crap. Crap wrapped in lies and dipped in bullshit."

"Gotcha." Lauren pointed to the men in the dumpster. "We're on a scavenger hunt, but we can step away for a bit if you need closure—"

"Closure?" She squinted at Lauren and shook her head from side to side. "Closure is for confused people. I know why it's over." She gave her friend a high five and stumbled a few steps toward the open dumpster. "Let's do this."

Lauren assumed the whole bin was going in the dumpster, but the friend placed it on the ground and removed the lid. The drunk coed leaned over the contents and lifted a shoebox out of the bin.

"I hate him." She took the top off the shoebox and flung it into the dumpster. It landed between Brenner and Scott. She shuffled through the items and said, "Birthday cards, spring break souvenirs, concert tickets, pictures." She lifted a photograph and waved it at her friend. She slurred her words when she asked her friend, "Know what really pisses me off?"

"What's that?"

"He's in *all* my pictures from college. Four years of parties, holidays, vacations, hanging out with friends." She held the photo in front of her face and swayed slightly. "All my pictures are ruined. I hate him."

"Let me help." Scott reached down from the dumpster and gestured for the box. "I hate him too."

She returned the photo to the stack and handed the shoebox to Scott. With a turn of his wrist, he dumped all the memories into the trash beside him. "Maybe you can Photoshop your pictures. Replace his face with Zac Efron or one of the Hemsworths."

She shook her head. "Jason Momoa."

Lauren nodded, and Ivy said, "I know that's right."

She looked at her friend and said, "And it's not like one day I could show my kids half of my college pictures anyway. They shouldn't see Mommy dressed like a slutty Stanley Cup two Halloweens in a row." She reached in the bin, grabbed a handful of silver lamé, and held up a strapless body-con tube dress. "I wore this tiny dress, silver stilettos, and a silver bowl on my head. It was forty degrees. He wore thick hockey pads and his Penguins jersey…lifted me in the air all night." She balled up the dress and threw it into the dumpster.

Her friend looked in the bin and said, "It happened a lot with you two. He's comfy as hell on Halloween, and you're half-naked and freezing." She picked up a gallon-size freezer bag from the plastic bin and stared at the contents. She rolled her eyes and handed it to her intoxicated friend.

One by one, the items were tossed into the dumpster. Lauren watched bunny ears, a bow tie, fishnet stockings, and a black leotard fly into the dumpster. The fuzzy bunny tail went in last. "Let me guess: he wore silk pajamas and a velvet smoking jacket."

"And the ridiculous captain's hat." She shook her head and said, "What was I thinking?" She reached in the bin for more fabric, unfurling the bottom half of a Princess Leia slave costume. She also grabbed the metal-edged bikini top, neck collar with chain, and hair accessories. "Yeah, I'm keeping this." The entire costume fell back into the bin. She replaced the lid and let out a sigh when it clicked closed.

The friend pulled her in for a hug and said, "Imagine how much more you'll love the right guy."

She nodded and returned the hug.

"He's lucky you're not vengeful." Scott looked at Brenner and asked, "Remember Hendrick?"

Brenner nodded. "Like I could forget."

"Hendrick was caught red-handed by his girlfriend." Scott laughed. Ivy glared at him, so he amended, "There's nothing funny about cheating. It's how his ex-girlfriend got even that makes me laugh."

"What'd she do?" asked Ivy.

"Rubbed poison ivy on all his briefs and socks."

"And shirts. And baseball caps," added Brenner. "And headphones."

"Wow." Lauren looked at Brenner with wide eyes. "How…thorough."

"She also poured spoiled milk under the floor mats in his Camaro," said Scott. "In July. In Alabama."

Ivy began a dramatic slow clap. "Respect."

Brenner laughed. "He found the poison ivy and sour milk the hard way."

"Wow," Lauren said. "It's like a Scared Straight program for cheaters."

The drunk woman turned to her friend. "I want to do something mean."

"Not too mean," the friend said. "I'm your ride or die, but let's not blow all our graduation money on bail tonight."

"Put glitter into his car's air vents or pour cooking oil in his windshield washer fluid." Scott gave her a thumbs up. "Or both."

Her friend said, "There's so much glitter in the Sigma's chapter room right now."

"Yes! Let's hurry!" After wishing Lauren luck in her scavenger hunt, they walked out of the dumpster enclosure.

Scott said, "I'm telling you: tonight is operating on a whole other level."

"Okay, where were we?" Brenner pointed to the paper clutched in Lauren's hand. "Are you using the letter or should we keep looking?"

Lauren had forgotten she was holding the letter. She unfolded it and read it a second time. "No, this works." She looked at Ivy and asked, "A love letter in a dumpster. Right?"

"It's perfect. Especially after watching that girl dump her relationship in the trash."

Lauren pulled up the photo she'd taken and sent it to the contest. "It's off to see the Wizard." Her phone went in her back pocket, and the letter floated back into the dumpster. "I hate throwing it away a second time."

"It's okay." Scott began climbing out of the dumpster. "I bet she wrote him hundreds of love letters. Poor guy couldn't keep track of them all."

Ivy smiled. "What a nice thought. Unlikely, but nice."

"Hey, it takes effort to send a handwritten note through snail mail. I bet she wrote him often while they were apart." Scott swung his other leg over the edge and jumped to the ground. "And I know he loved checking the mail every day."

Brenner followed Scott up and over the side of the dumpster. When he was back on the concrete pad, he bent at the waist to brush away tiny pieces of Styrofoam clinging to his jeans.

"I hope you guys didn't get too filthy in there," Lauren said.

"It wasn't too bad. I have soap and water in my ruck, some clean shirts too."

Ivy stepped down from the mini fridge and stood close to Scott. "You don't smell like hot trash."

"Sweet talker." Scott winked and removed his gloves. "It wasn't messy in there, just plastic bags and boxes mostly."

"Don't forget Magic Mike and Robert Plant," said Brenner.

Scott picked up the bowling pin lamp and said, "Or this beauty."

Lauren handed Brenner his flashlight. "Thanks again for driving out here and helping me."

"It was my pleasure, truly."

Ivy took Scott's hand and led him out of the enclosure. "Let's walk back to the cars and wait for the next adventure." They discussed their first and second dates while Lauren and Brenner followed several steps back.

"Here we go again," Brenner said with a laugh. Gesturing toward the couple before them, he said, "I promise we'll get to the next hashtag quickly."

"Thank you." Lauren laughed and said, "It'd be obnoxious if they weren't so adorable." After a few steps, her smile faded and her forehead creased with concern. "Do you think I should have sent a picture of the bowling pin lamp?"

"No way." Brenner stopped walking and gently reached for Lauren's wrist. Once she was standing still in front of him, he continued. "The love letter's a slam dunk. Way better than the bottom half of an ugly lamp."

"Right. Okay," Lauren said, taking a deep breath. "Thanks. This one was different from the rest, and I've been second-guessing myself since I sent the picture. The other hashtags were hard to find, but there was no mistaking what the Wizard wanted."

They resumed walking, and Brenner asked, "What else have you tracked down tonight?"

"In order: parachute pants, dinosaur novelty socks, Santa Claus, a man bun…" She looked at Brenner and felt her face get hot. "Hottie in the wild."

"And a dumpster dive find." Brenner nodded. "Wait. Did you say Santa Claus?"

Lauren nodded and said, "Yep. Santa."

"It's almost summer." Brenner laughed and looked at Lauren. "Where did you find Santa Claus?"

"Actually, he was the easiest one so far. I went to Jefe's in Piper Glen. Have you been?"

"No. I moved here a few weeks ago."

"Oh." She was surprised his recent move had not come up in conversation yet. Or maybe it had, and she missed it by staring at her phone all night. "Well then, welcome to the Queen City." She wanted to ask him personal questions about where he was from and what brought him to Charlotte, but instead, she pulled her phone out of her pocket and opened her photo gallery. "Jefe's is my favorite Mexican restaurant. Thanks to Taco Tuesday, I am well acquainted with the life-size Santa on display year-round. He's in the waiting area next to the Christmas tree they decorate all year."

"They celebrate Christmas all year long?"

"Not just Christmas, no. The story goes, the owners' young kids didn't want to take down the decorations, so they put New Year's Eve decorations on the tree and dressed Santa up in a tux. Then it was Valentine's Day with hearts on the tree, and Santa had a pink suit and a red bow tie." As she thumbed through the photos on her phone, Lauren laughed and said, "Then shamrocks and he got a leprechaun costume… You get the idea."

"First of all, you had me at 'Taco Tuesday,' and a life-size Santa dressed as a leprechaun? This I have to see."

"Over the years, it's become a fun tradition." She showed Brenner the photo she'd submitted a few hours ago.

"These days, Santa's celebrating Cinco de Mayo."

Brenner took her phone and zoomed in on a picture of a six-foot plastic Santa wearing a straw sombrero and a colorful serape layered over a white shirt and blue jeans. Zip ties secured an empty Corona bottle to one hand and a Mexican flag to the other.

"Awesome."

"Right? I was worried the Wizard would only accept the traditional Christmas Santa Claus, but Jefe's got me to the next hashtag." When Brenner handed her phone back, Lauren realized this was the most extended conversation they'd had since meeting at Barkley's.

"Wonder what they do for June," Brenner said as they reached the parking lot. "We'll have to go so I can see for myself."

"Where are we going?" asked Scott. He and Ivy were leaning against Brenner's truck, watching Lauren and Brenner.

"This Mexican restaurant Lauren was telling me about," Brenner said. "They have Taco Tuesday and a seasonal Santa."

"Oh yeah, Jefe's," Ivy said. "Lauren goes there almost every week."

"Thanks, Ivy," Lauren said with a smirk. She checked her phone for a text from the Wizard, surprised at herself for not having tested a dozen times by now.

"Heard anything yet?" Scott asked.

Lauren said, "No, but I'm hopeful."

"I bet your Wizard is zooming in on the picture and reading the letter right now."

"I hope you're right," Lauren said, looking from Scott to Brenner.

Brenner looked at his watch. "The contest ends at five in the morning?"

"Yes. We're going to need some coffee. I'll buy us—" Realizing what she'd been about to imply, Lauren startled and said, "Sorry! I'm acting like you are hanging with us all night, but we got the dumpster find photo. You guys should go back to Barkley's or go home or…"

"Are you serious?" Scott said. "This is the best night ever!" He raised Ivy's hand and the bowling pin in the air. "I met this lovely lady and scored this sweet lamp. The last thing I want to do is go home. I want to help you win this contest."

"Same here." Brenner looked her in the eyes and said, "Unless you flat out tell us to leave, we're hanging with you all night."

Lauren looked down. "I don't want you to think you have to stay."

"I don't want you to think I want to leave." He leaned against her car and said, "I may not be as obnoxious as Scott, but I'm also having a blast tonight."

"Oh, okay." Lauren offered a shy smile, hoping Brenner would know it was genuine.

CHAPTER EIGHT

Brenner

"**P**LEASE SAY WE CAN STAY." SCOTT POUTED AND BATTED his eyelashes. "In all honesty, this is the most fun I've had since coming home."

"How long have you been back?" Ivy asked.

Scott looked at his watch. "About seven hours now."

Ivy sprung off Brenner's truck and stood up straight. "Seven hours? Hours?"

"Yeah, I flew in earlier today."

"Where were you?"

"It's a long story." Scott winked at Ivy. "I'll tell you all about it on our third date."

Ivy laughed. "Deal. But at least tell me where you boarded the plane that landed in Charlotte."

"The last leg was out of London."

Ivy gasped.

"Wait." Lauren jumped into their conversation. "You were in London today, and you're out here tonight?"

"Absolutely I'm out here tonight," Scott said as he squeezed Ivy's hand. "Besides, I'm still on Europe time. I slept on the plane earlier, so I'm wide awake now."

Ivy looked at Brenner and said, "What about you? Did you leave London today?"

"No, my flight landed weeks ago." He nodded toward Scott and said, "His first order of business after landing was meeting up at Barkley's."

"And you're welcome." Scott looked at Lauren and said, "My text saved him from slipping into a couch coma."

"Sully, I was eating pizza and watching Netflix."

"I rest my case."

"Anyway," Brenner turned toward Lauren and asked, "do you have something specific in mind for this prize money you're going to win?"

Lauren rested her hip against her car and angled her body a bit toward him before she answered. "Yes, I have something particular in mind."

Brenner mirrored her stance, so they were both propped against her car and facing each other.

Lauren's text alert went off, and she didn't immediately look at her phone. When she finally glanced down, her smile only grew.

"Is it from the Wizard?" asked Brenner.

"Hashtag accepted." She angled the phone so he could read the text, but his eyes never left her smile.

"Told you."

"Yes, you did." Brenner watched as Lauren closed the Wizard's text and opened the #HashtagHunt app. She bit her lip as the leaderboard refreshed. Once the updated list appeared, she slumped against her car and held her phone to her chest with both hands. "Still in second place."

Genuinely happy for her, Brenner lifted his hand for a high five from Lauren. She freely smacked her palm against his and he realized he wanted to see Lauren again after this contest was over. Their conversation after the dumpster find wasn't forced or uncomfortable, and he looked forward to knowing her better. She was kind and intelligent, and her honesty was refreshing. He smiled at the irony, knowing they had only met because she was caught taking his picture behind his back.

"Excuse me!" Ivy looked from Lauren to Brenner and back to Lauren. Gesturing toward Scott, she said, "Don't leave us hanging!" She pointed to Lauren's phone and asked, "You get a text or what?"

"Oh! Yes!"

"From the Wizard?" Lauren nodded, and Ivy rolled her eyes. "And what does it say?"

"Right! Sorry." After sneaking a glance at Brenner, Lauren awkwardly pushed herself off the car door to face Ivy. She retrieved the text and read it aloud.

Challenge 7 of 12: #OldSchool
Time Remaining: 7 hours and 01 minutes

"Old school?" Scott slapped his hands together. "This one sounds like fun."

"More fun than old trash anyway," said Ivy.

"You are officially three for three." Lauren rushed toward Ivy and hugged her.

Ivy said, "Let's keep this momentum going!" She lifted her phone out of her purse and leaned against Brenner's truck next to Scott. "Let's see what Pinterest has to offer for 'old school.'"

Scott set the lamp down near his feet and tugged his phone out of his pocket. "Good thinking. Pinterest has everything."

Ivy laughed but didn't look up from her phone. "And you know this how?"

"I have sisters," he said with a shrug. "One of them owns a third-floor walk-up in Queens but saves pictures of walk-in closets and infinity pools."

"She sounds awesome." Ivy showed Scott her phone screen as she scrolled through the images. "Fisher-Price toys, eighties fashion, mixed tapes, Trapper Keepers…" She stopped scrolling and tapped on a picture. "Record players!" She looked at Lauren and said, "Send a picture of your turntable and record collection."

Lauren looked up from her screen. "Um, I don't know. Not sure it's old school enough."

"Record collection?" Brenner asked.

Lauren smiled at Brenner before returning her eyes to her phone. "I was the only one in my family who wanted my grandpa's vinyl records when he died. Adding to the collection became a hobby."

"I have friends who collect records. They say vinyl sounds and smells better than any download."

Lauren laughed. "True."

"We could go back to Barkley's." Ivy kept scrolling on her phone. "Jess has her old Polaroid camera behind the bar."

Lauren shook her head. "I don't think it should be something anyone can find in a home or a pawn shop." Ivy looked confused, and Lauren continued. "I want to send the Wizard something as fast as possible, but retro relics from the eighties seem too obvious. Too easy."

Scott was also searching on his phone. "I'm finding old cartoon characters and action figures."

"This could be another subjective challenge," Brenner

said to Lauren. "When I saw '#OldSchool' on your phone, I thought hip-hop. Graffiti. Break dancing. Run-DMC with tracksuits, adidas, and heavy chains."

"Yes!" Ivy lowered her phone and said, "Resend your picture of Feral Meryl break-dancing!"

Lauren laughed and said, "I wish I could, but no repeats allowed."

"Your picture of who now?" asked Brenner. "A feral break-dancer?"

"Hold up." Scott looked at Lauren. "Feral Meryl's still around?" She nodded, and he said, "Good Lord, she will outlive us all. Why'd you need her picture?"

"The first hashtag was parachute pants."

"Nice!" Scott nodded. "I should go see her." He elbowed Ivy's arm. "Date number four? A picnic in Center City Park? Watch some break dancing?"

Brenner stopped leaning against Lauren's car and took a few steps toward the redbrick buildings surrounding the parking lot, taking in the classic architecture. "Regents College is an old school." He pointed to the "Founded in 1857" sign next to the building beside the parking lot.

Lauren looked up from her phone and seemed to considered the dorms and classrooms scattered throughout the campus. She squinted when she said, "I think the only original buildings left are the chapel and admin building, but I like where you're going with this." Suddenly, she stood up straight, snapped her fingers, and looked at Ivy. Lauren said, "The abandoned schoolhouse on four nineteen!"

Ivy laughed. "We go from mounds of trash to a haunted death trap?"

"Yeah."

"Haunted death trap? Sign me up!" said Scott. "How

do I not know about this?"

"It was set to be demolished, but historical preservation folks moved it out to four nineteen to restore." Ivy shrugged. "They ran out of money, so it's rotting away. Total death trap."

"But it has faded red paint and a bell tower and everything." Lauren looked at Brenner and Scott. "It's straight out of *Little House on the Prairie*."

"And what makes it haunted?" asked Brenner.

"Some ghost stories were passed around after a few high school parties," said Lauren. "I'm sure they had more to do with cheap booze than paranormal activity."

Ivy asked, "What if we drive way out there and find an empty lot?"

"I think it's worth the trip to get something different from random retro stuff. We can think of a plan B on the way there."

"Lauren's right." Brenner unlocked his truck. "The Wizard will appreciate the effort, and it is literally an old school, so she'll have to accept it. It's worth the extra time to get the photo. You'll definitely level up."

"Yes, right." Lauren fished in her purse for her car keys. "Do you guys want to follow us there?"

Scott picked up the bowling pin lamp from the ground and set it into the bed of Brenner's truck. "Where on four nineteen is it?"

Lauren pulled up the location on her phone and showed it to Scott. "I know a shortcut that'll save us at least ten minutes," he said.

"What shortcut?" asked Ivy.

"We go through Underwood Farms instead of all the way around it."

"Underwood Farms… The pumpkin patch place?" asked Lauren.

Scott nodded. "Pumpkins, apples, hayrides, huge corn maze."

"But it doesn't open until the fall," Ivy said. "And it's private property. We're avoiding trespassing charges, remember?"

Scott put his hand on Ivy's shoulder. "The Underwoods are family friends," said Scott. "They'll be fine with it, but it's better to ask for one vehicle to drive through their farm. We should ride together." He tapped on his phone's screen before raising the phone to his ear. "I'll give them a heads-up so they don't shoot us on sight." He turned his back when someone picked up. "Wyatt? Hey, man! Yeah, I just got back today. So, I'm sorry to call so late…oh…no, no. Nothing's wrong, but do you have a minute?" Scott walked away from Brenner's truck as he spoke. "I need a favor." He distanced himself from the group to continue the call.

Ivy said, "Normally, we would never get into a car with guys we just met. But you guys waded through trash for us."

"Wait…I can't leave my car here," Lauren said. "Can I?"

"I think it'll be fine," said Brenner. "The visitors' lot is well lit. There are surveillance cameras, and campus police will make their rounds."

Lauren looked around the parking lot and quiet college campus.

"I'm sure it'll be fine for an hour or so," said Ivy.

Scott returned from his brief walk and settled in next to Ivy. "We're all set. Got the code to the gate and everything." He put his phone in his pocket and told Lauren, "They were more than happy to help and wish you luck on your contest."

"Then let's get going," said Brenner.

Ivy moved to stand near Lauren. "And you guys swear you're not serial killers?"

Scott rubbed the back of his neck and asked Brenner, "She means in a noncombatant kind of way, right?"

"Ignore him." Brenner laughed and shook his head. "How about this: send pictures of our IDs and my license plate to a friend."

"Good idea." Ivy held out her palm. "Hand them over."

Brenner pulled his wallet out of his back pocket and handed his driver's license to Ivy. As she passed it to Lauren, Scott's fingers curled around a silver chain previously concealed by his clothing. He tugged the dog tags from under his shirt, then over his head, and then slowly lowered them on Ivy's open palm.

"Come on, Sully." Brenner rolled his eyes. "Quit showing off."

"What do you mean?" Scott asked with a smile. "As far as identification goes, it works."

"Oh, it's working all right." Ivy stared at the ball chain necklace covering the metal tags in her hand.

Lauren tried to cover her laugh with a cough as she took a picture of Brenner's license. She returned it to him and made her way to the back of his truck. "This photo doesn't do you justice."

Brenner laughed. "Thanks." He followed her and returned the license to his wallet. Propping an elbow on the tailgate, he said, "Nobody looks as bad as their DMV photo or as good as their profile pic."

"So true." Lauren laughed. "I'm sending your ID and plate to our friend Amy." As she typed, she nodded toward Scott and Ivy. "I don't think we need his, and I'd hate to interrupt the flirtfest."

"It's unlike him to flash the dog tags at a lady, but Ivy seems to like them."

"She does have a weakness for military men."

"Let me guess…because of the uniform?"

"Because they follow orders," Lauren joked. "The camo and dog tags don't hurt though."

Lauren and Brenner walked back to where their friends were standing, and Ivy was using her phone's torch light to read the raised letters on Scott's dog tags. She said, "I'm O positive too!"

"Well, I've known you were my type for a while now."

"Ugh," Ivy groaned. "So lame." Ivy returned the dog tags to Scott. "You'll have to explain sometime why 'None' is your religious preference."

"It makes for great conversation on date number… What are we up to now? Five?" Scott opened the truck's passenger-side rear door for Ivy. "As much as I'd love to join you back here, I have to sit up front. These long legs get a little stiff sometimes."

"A little?" Brenner rolled his eyes. "Sometimes?" On the other side of the truck, he opened the rear door for Lauren. As she climbed into the truck, he asked, "Did Amy get your text?"

"Yes, and she already texted back." Lauren settled into the rear cab and reached for the seat belt. "She's going to check in with us from time to time to make sure we're okay."

"She's a good friend."

"She's the best."

Brenner shut Lauren's door at the same time Scott closed Ivy's. The friends looked at each other across the roof of the truck. "You can thank me later," Scott said. "Let's get your girl another hashtag."

Once everyone was in the truck, Ivy said, "We've got seven hours to finish the contest. No telling what else is up the Wizard's sleeve."

Brenner cranked the engine and put the truck in gear. "The best things are unexpected." He caught Lauren's eyes in the rearview mirror and said, "I'm excited to see where tonight takes us."

CHAPTER NINE

Lauren

AS HE TURNED OUT OF THE PARKING LOT, IVY LEANED forward and held out her open palm to Brenner. "Let's see your dog tags, soldier."

"I keep them at home."

"Why?" Ivy settled back into her seat. "Don't you need them?"

"I do when I'm on base or active duty." Brenner turned his head toward Scott. "I only wear them with my uniform." He looked forward as he steered his truck onto the road. "But my middle initial is M, my blood type is A negative, and I'm a nondenominational Christian."

Scott twisted to face the women in the backseat. "I tried to get him to put 'Druid' or 'Jedi' as his religion, but he's no fun."

"Says the guy who put 'None,'" said Ivy.

"Look, if I'm dead, I don't care what kind of send-off Uncle Sam gives me," Scott said with a shrug. "Might as well make it easier for clergy scrambling to give last rites to Wiccans and whatnot."

Brenner raised his right hand off the steering wheel.

"This is a bit of a sensitive subject for Sully." He looked at Ivy over his right shoulder. "And you're discussing why he chose 'None' on one of your dozens of dates, right?"

"Right," said Ivy and Scott at the same time. Ivy reached forward to pat Scott's left shoulder. Before she could remove her hand, he covered it with his and gently squeezed.

Lauren witnessed Scott and Ivy convey a silent truce through flexed fingers as they both looked out their own window. Her gaze left Scott's shoulder and traveled to the rearview mirror. Her eyes met Brenner's. Again. Suddenly shy, she turned her head to stare out her window on her left. Not much of a view, but she studied a long line of condos under construction down from the college. Without warning, memories of Josh flooded her mind.

Her last relationship, like the handful before it, had started off strong. Mutual. Effortless. In time, however, the scales became unbalanced. Lauren's heart sank as the affection on the other side of the scale lost its substance. Sometimes it was a gradual decline. Sometimes she plummeted when the counterweight was removed all at once. Some hearts were equipped with an on/off switch for feelings, but hers was not. She was incapable of forgetting the select few she had deeply loved. She saved a quiet corner of her heart for whitewashed memories of the ones who found their balance elsewhere.

After Josh, Lauren set aside a few weeks to grieve lost love. What had been an excruciating heartbreak faded to a dull ache. She was over him but still missed what they almost had. She probably always would.

Over the past few months, Lauren had embraced her single status, free to reign over every detail of her life. She didn't seek approval before joining the Hashtag Hunt, and she didn't explain how joining a crazy contest trumped borrowing Ivy's money.

Naturally, since Lauren loved her life as is, she'd meet a man like Brenner. She was torn between the excitement of getting to know more about him and the inevitable frustration of when he'd eventually lose interest… But she was getting way ahead of herself. Other than some eye contact, a couple of flirty comments, and what appeared to be genuine interest in Jefe's Santa Claus, Brenner was playing it cool. Unlike Scott, who Lauren guessed would pop the question on date number eleven.

Lauren shook her head to clear her thoughts. This was not the time to remember guys who had broken her heart or to make more out of her time with Brenner than necessary. She forced her brain to focus on Scott's voice as he navigated the truck to the gated entrance of Underwood Farms. Once she was refocused on the contest, Lauren checked her phone for updates. Nothing new on the app, but her phone lit up with a new text alert. So did Ivy's. It was from Amy, using the same three-way text thread the friends had used for years.

Amy: Checking in. If you don't reply in five minutes, I'm calling 911.

Despite having just received the text, Lauren's thumbs flew across the keyboard. Ivy also started texting on her phone.

Lauren: All is well! Stand down! No cops.

Ivy: But good looking out. Ty

Amy: Np

Amy: I see you're holding down second place, L.

Ivy: Right? !!!! SO excited!

Lauren: But only halfway through the hashtags.
Lauren: …and only 7 hours left.

"Look at them, hunched over their phones," said Scott.

"Amy demanded signs of life," said Ivy. "We're telling her we're safe…for now."

"She's already checking in with you?" asked Brenner. "It's been ten minutes."

"Not sure serial killers work so fast," joked Scott. "Although if we'd used chloroform or ether, you'd be unable to text back… So props to her."

"Chloroform or ether?" asked Ivy. "That only happens on TV."

"When the show is set in the 1850s," said Brenner. Everyone in the truck laughed, including Scott.

"So I'm not current on the most effective abduction techniques. This should go in the plus column." Scott shrugged and pointed to the road ahead. "The entrance will be on the right. Half a mile or so."

Lauren's phone lit up with another text.

Amy: Proud of you.
Amy: You got this.
Ivy: Damn straight.
Ivy: Oh! And guess what else she's got?
Amy: ??
Ivy: The hottie from #5 is driving us in his…
Ivy: Big. Black. Truck.
Amy: Holllla!!!
Amy: Wait. What?
Ivy: #HitW is the one driving.
Amy: …but the H stands for "hottie," right?
Ivy: ???

Lauren: Stand by…

Lauren texted the #HitW photo to Amy and Ivy.

Lauren: ^ what he really looks like.
Amy: Oh haiii!!!
Amy: Much better.

Ivy angled her phone toward Lauren. "What's she talking about?"

Lauren could not contain her laugh. She backed out of the group text and tapped on the messages between just her and Amy. Lauren enlarged the picture of Brenner's driver's license and zoomed in on his photo. She passed her phone to Ivy, who gasped.

Scott turned around to face them. "Everything okay?"

"Brenner, what did you do to upset the DMV photographer?" Ivy failed at keeping the humor out of her voice. She returned Lauren's phone and laughed.

"What am I missing?" asked Scott.

"Amy didn't believe our driver was Lauren's hottie. And after seeing his DMV photo, I understand the confusion."

"Oh, really?" Scott rubbed his palms together. "This I gotta see." He leaned across the armrest between him and Brenner and said, "Let's see your driver's license, soldier."

"Get off me." Brenner shoved Scott back to the passenger side of the cab. "It's not that bad, people!"

"Let's agree to disagree," said Ivy with a giggle.

"That's what you're texting about back there?" Brenner looked in the rearview mirror. "My DMV photo?"

"I'm relieved they're discussing your ugly mug." Scott turned to Ivy. "I thought you were Googling how to dispose of our bodies after you murder us at the haunted schoolhouse."

"Yeah, but first I'd have to Google how to travel back in time and buy ether." Ivy patted Scott's shoulder again. "Relax, handsome. Nobody in this truck will be chopped into itty-bitty pieces tonight."

Lauren rolled her eyes at the ridiculousness of the conversation. A quick glance at her phone revealed a few more texts from Amy.

Amy: If you don't make me a clone of the hottie, I will never speak to you again.

Amy: Jk

Amy: Kinda.

Amy: $10K AND a hot man AND a black truck?

Amy: Christmas came early for you, girl!

Lauren: None of those things are mine.

Ivy: Yet.

Amy: ^ what she said.

Amy: And where is the hottie driving you?

Ivy: To #7 - Old School.

Amy: ??

Amy: Ivy - I thought you were seeing Scottie E.

Ivy: I'm helping L instead.

Lauren: She's been a huge help.

Lauren: Also, the hottie has an Army friend wearing dog tags.

Amy: Say no more.

Ivy: We're going to the movie tomorrow.

Ivy: !!!

Amy: Does the hottie have any more friends in his big, black truck?

Lauren: LOL - afraid not.

Lauren: We're almost to the pumpkin farm. Gotta go.

Amy: I thought you said Old School.

Lauren: Long story. You'll hear it all asap. Promise.

Amy: I'll text you later to make sure all is well. Stay safe.

Ivy: Thanks, A!

Lauren: Love you, girl.

Amy: Love you more.

Brenner signaled right and turned his truck onto a gravel road. For several yards, rocks crunched beneath the tires before the entrance to Underwood Farms came into view. A massive wrought iron gate extended the length of the road and the truck's headlamps illuminated the intricate details welded into the structure: pumpkins and vines, cornstalks and haystacks, wagon wheels, hearts, butterflies. A large capital *U* sat prominently in the center, surrounded by decorative scrolls and maple leaves. Lauren had been so distracted admiring the craftsmanship, she didn't realize Scott was on the phone until she heard his voice.

"Yeah, man. We're here." Scott opened the passenger door and leaped out of the truck while holding the phone to his ear. Lauren didn't hear what else was said, but the conversation continued as Scott approached the keypad, entered the code, and unlocked the metal gate. He ended the call and pushed the gate, sweeping it across the gravel. Once the opening was wide enough, Brenner drove onto the property.

When the truck passed him, Scott swung the gate closed. The massive structure traveled quickly, and the brash clang of wrought iron and the ensuing metallic rattling made Lauren jump in the backseat. Brenner ducked low in his seat and hit the gas, zigzagging down the road and spitting gravel in his wake. Ivy screamed until the truck stopped thirty yards ahead of where it had been idling. The three of them turned around to look through the back window at Scott.

"Damn it, B!" Scott wiped the dust from his eyes. "What the hell?"

Brenner put the truck in reverse, watched the rearview camera, and slowly drove backward in a straight line. "I'm sorry, ladies." His voice was thick with embarrassment. "When the gate closed, it sounded like…artillery fire, and…swerving is an evasive maneuver. It was a knee-jerk reaction." He cleared his throat. "Sully will never let me hear the end of this."

Scott was headed toward the truck, wiping the dust off his jeans. He had only walked a few feet when he abruptly halted his steps. He raised his left fist in the air, giving Brenner some type of hand signal. The brake lights cast Scott in an ominous red glow.

"What's happening?" Ivy whispered as she grabbed Lauren's hand.

Brenner said, "He heard something out there."

The sides of the entrance were covered with tall ornamental grasses, resulting in a naturalistic border to the property. Lauren watched Scott slowly turn his head to the left and stare into the long blades of grass. Suddenly, the tips bent under the weight of a whitetail deer as it jumped through the plants, nearly clearing the six-foot hedge. Despite its graceful landing, the buck became skittish when it saw Scott. In an uncoordinated attack, the startled deer leaped sideways and swung its stubby, velvet-covered antlers from side to side.

Ivy's scream was deafening in the cab of the truck, and Lauren was frozen in fear. Brenner threw his vehicle back in gear and inched forward as he rolled down his window. He gave a low whistle, put his arm out the window and waved Scott forward. When the deer lowered its head and kicked its hind legs, Brenner shouted, "Run, Sully!"

Scott bolted in the direction of the truck. The buck kept pace with him before rearing back in a fighting stance. Its front feet punched through the air, narrowly missing Scott's torso, but caught on the fabric of his jeans. Sharp hooves ripped the denim below Scott's left knee as the animal dropped to all fours. Scott yelled, "Go! Go!" Brenner hit the gas and sped down the road. Gravel pelted the underbody and sprayed out from the tires. Scott outran the deer and dodged the rocks for a few steps before jumping over ten feet, landing in the bed of Brenner's truck.

Lauren could have dismissed the leap as a staggering display of athleticism or dumb luck, but the height, distance, and speed at which Scott soared defied belief. After coming down near the center of the truck bed, he slid backward and slammed into the tailgate. Brenner reduced his speed after the impact, but Scott continued to bounce with the movement of the truck traveling over the gravel. He was in a ball with both arms wrapped around his head. Lauren looked at Ivy, who stared at Scott with wide, unblinking eyes.

From the front seat, Brenner asked, "Do you see the deer?"

Lauren squinted at the view behind the truck. It took a moment to find her voice, and even when she did, it came out as a breathless whisper. "No." She cleared her throat, and a bit louder said, "No, it's gone."

CHAPTER TEN

Brenner

BRENNER STOPPED THE TRUCK AND TOOK SEVERAL DEEP breaths, trying to slow his heart rate. After checking his side and rearview mirrors, he confirmed the buck was no longer following them. He put the truck in park and grabbed his flashlight. He opened his door and said, "I know we're in a hurry, but I need to make sure he's alright." He glanced over his shoulder to gauge Lauren's and Ivy's level of shock. They were staring at Scott through the cab's back window. Their rigid posture and baffled silence told Brenner all he needed to know.

He clicked on the flashlight and hurried to the back of the truck. Brenner lowered the tailgate and aimed the light on Scott, who was unfolding his arms and legs from the fetal position. "You bleeding on my truck, man?"

Scott groaned as he rolled and lifted his torso to a sitting position.

"We don't have time for the ER." Brenner jutted his chin at the bowling pin near Scott's feet. "At least you didn't land on the lamp. You didn't stick the landing, but you're in one piece. A silver lining, right?"

"B, you and your silver lining can go pound sand." Scott rubbed his right shoulder and stared at the rip in his jeans. The silver casing of the bionic leg was visible through the torn denim, and its metallic finish reflected the light Brenner was shining on him. "Damn buck." Scott held his hand out for the flashlight. "If he cracked any of the polymer, I will track that animal down." He focused the light on the area below his knee and ran his fingertips over the superficial scratches in the metal.

"A one-year warranty isn't one of the perks?"

"Shut up." Scott laughed and swung his legs over the edge of the tailgate. "Guess I can add 'gets major air' to my rapidly growing list of perks." He arched and stretched his back. "Any chance Ivy didn't see?"

"Didn't see what?" Brenner pointed to a spot twenty feet down the road. "Your supernatural Lambeau Leap?" Then he pointed at Scott's leg. "Or the sci-fi soldier gear?"

"Either." Scott shrugged. "Both."

"I'm pretty sure she saw it all." Brenner peeked at the women in his truck. "They both did."

"Fantastic." Scott turned off the flashlight and returned it to Brenner. "At least I had a few hours of normalcy with her."

"Sully." Brenner rolled his eyes. "None of the time you've spent together tonight has been normal."

"Yeah. You might have a point there."

"And if it makes you feel any better, Lauren and Ivy had front row seats for my reaction of the gate slamming shut." Brenner had been mortified by his behavior but knew this wasn't the time or place for his issues. He shelved the embarrassment. For now. He'd break the habits picked up on deployment. Eventually. "I could have done without an audience for my freak show."

"Your embarrassment would make me feel better if I hadn't been pelted with gravel when you hauled ass." Scott slid off the tailgate. "Leaving me in the dust to arm-wrestle a twelve-point buck with my bare hands."

"Twelve point—" Brenner leaned back and laughed. "Yeah, okay. Leave out the 'taking on enemy fire' part and I'll confirm it was the mightiest stag in the land."

"Deal." Scott rounded the back of the truck and knocked on Ivy's window with a knuckle. "This is going to be awkward."

"Good luck, brother." Brenner walked in the other direction and sat in the driver's seat.

Ivy lowered her electric window. "Well, aren't you chock-full of surprises."

"Thanks?"

She reached through the window and put her hand on his arm. "Between the deer jumping out of nowhere and you...jumping in the truck, I may be in shock."

"That makes four of us." Scott leaned against Ivy's door. "And now I smell like hot trash and a wild animal."

"Are you hurt?"

"I ruptured my pride, but it always grows back."

Ivy shook her head. "You have a metal leg?"

"Well, I have two metal legs." Scott closed his eyes and rubbed his chin. "I'll miss you looking at me like I'm whole, and I won't like you looking at me like I'm not. I know we need to get going, but before I get in the truck, I need you to promise me something."

Ivy leaned out her window and looked up at him. "Promise what?"

Scott opened his eyes. "Do not feel sorry for me."

"I don't—"

"Hang on. Let me explain: I've spent the past year surrounded by doctors and scientists determined to fix me. Help me. Improve me."

"Scott." Ivy smiled up at him. "Listen: am I surprised you have two metal legs? Yeah. Sure I am. Was it shocking when you landed in the back of the truck like you'd been shot out of a cannon? Hell yes."

"I—"

"Hang on. Let *me* explain: I have a thousand questions, but none of them are, 'Do you need my help, Scott?' I can promise I don't feel sorry for you. In fact, you get around better than anyone I know."

"I'll answer all of your questions." Scott cleared his throat. "There is also the other end of the spectrum: you think I'm a hero...or prosthetics are a turn-on."

Ivy laughed, but then suddenly stopped and said, "Oh, you're serious." She looked at Brenner and Lauren before returning her eyes to Scott. "You lost your legs while in the Army? In combat?"

"Yes, and yes."

"Then I do think you're a hero, and sorry if it's a deal-breaker." Ivy sat back in her seat. "Get in the truck, Scott. We can discuss my list of turn-ons later."

"There's a list?"

"Yes."

"Can I see it?"

"Maybe."

Scott opened Ivy's door and leaned into the backseat of the cab. "Lauren, I know it's not a shortcut if it takes twice as long to get there, but I'm going to need one more minute."

"Take your time." In the rearview mirror, Brenner saw Lauren smile as she turned her head to look out her window. "Make it count."

Brenner followed suit and looked out the driver's window. Averting their eyes gave Scott and Ivy a small amount of privacy, but at least it was something. Scott's voice was soft but carried well in the truck cab. "Ivy, I should be a gentleman and wait until after an official second date to kiss you, but what if another deer attacks me before I get the chance?"

"Jump over it?"

"Smart-ass."

Brenner and Lauren chuckled and pretended they didn't hear their friends' first kiss or Scott's words after it was over. "I don't know where you came from, but now you're here... God, Ivy. It's like when stars are born after gravity and pressure squeeze atoms until they break apart, and suddenly there's enough light and heat to sustain life."

"I don't follow, but you had me after 'when stars are born.'"

"Look up at the stars for a second."

Brenner knew Scott was talking to Ivy, but it didn't stop him from looking at the night sky. He didn't check to see, but he imagined Lauren was also gazing up out her window.

"Fast Astronomy 101 lesson: darkness can get so dense and deep it changes everything. Atoms. People. Families. Countries. With enough pressure, the only place energy can go is outward and upward."

The truck was quiet for a moment before Ivy spoke. "I understand darkness and pressure changing things. But then where does the light come from?"

"Interstellar clouds. Watch this, guys."

Brenner turned to watch Scott through Ivy's door. A quick peek in his rearview mirror revealed Lauren had also turned to look. Scott pointed with his index finger and moved it in a full oval shape. "Let's say the cloud starts off this big. It swirls around because of gravity." Scott moved his finger, and the oval got smaller with each trip toward his shirt. "Gravity makes the cloud close in on itself as it turns." The oval he was making became so small, only the tip of his finger twirled in a tight circle. "When it's compact and dense enough, a nuclear reaction occurs." Scott curled his finger into his palm and made a fist. "The reaction produces heat and light, and a star is born." He popped his fist open and spread his fingers wide. "Basically like a furnace."

"Where do the clouds come from?" Ivy asked as she made a wide oval with her finger.

"They're made up of hydrogen gas and dust."

"Where do the gas and dust come from?"

"Ah, they're scattered all over outer space."

"But where do they come from?"

"Other stars dying out... Which I know is a type of chicken-and-egg answer."

Ivy lowered her gaze from the stars and focused on Scott. "And like the chicken and the egg, which do you think came first?"

"Jury's still out." Scott stepped back and closed Ivy's door. The window was still rolled down, and through the opening, he said, "Open minds have the best views."

"I can live with that."

Scott opened his door and sat in the passenger seat. When he fastened his seat belt, he looked at Brenner.

"Wyatt said to follow this road until we reach the pond. There'll be a fork in the road, and we go left."

Brenner gave Scott the side-eye as he started the engine and put the truck in gear.

"What?" Scott shifted in his seat to face Brenner. "You got a problem turning left at the pond?"

"Sully. Are we seriously going to act like that didn't happen?"

"Can you be more specific?" Scott laughed. "Many things have happened since we got here."

"True, but even more shocking than a deer attack or you jumping into the back of a moving truck was your pop-up lecture on how stars are born."

"I am wooing my special lady friend. And it's a solid metaphor, if I do say so myself." Scott twisted further to look at Ivy. "You liked it, right, Sweets?"

"Loved it. Nobody's ever compared me to a nuclear reaction before."

"Shameful." Scott winked at Ivy. "And there's more where that came from."

Brenner shook his head and resumed driving. "I've known you a long time, and I have never heard you even mention outer space...except when you'd give Woodson shit for watching sci-fi on base."

"Ugh. Of all the shows to download on a laptop, Woodson brought five seasons of *Andromeda*. But the real-deal outer space is a lot more interesting than any sci-fi soap opera on cable."

"No arguments there."

"Look, between operations, I had quite a bit of time on my hands, B." Stretching his legs out in front of him, Scott said, "I shared a room with an Airman First Class who lost his arm below the elbow. He wanted to work for NASA and was always reading books and magazines about astronomy. He was getting his master's in physical science. Smart kid who rattled off fun facts about outer space in his sleep." Scott looked at Brenner. "I never complained because at least someone was having sweet dreams."

"Lucky kid." Brenner laughed and said, "Except for the part where he lost an arm and roomed with you in the hospital."

"Well, we can't have everything, right? Anyway, one night I was lying there listening to how many Earths fit in the sun and what 'spaghettified' means, when he said Mars has a volcano that's sixteen miles high."

Brenner couldn't conceal his shock. "What?"

"A volcano. Sixteen. Miles. High. It was all I could think about that night, and at the time I was grateful for the distraction, ya know?" Scott gestured toward his legs. "In the morning I asked him if that particular stat was accurate. He said not only is the volcano sixteen miles high, but it's also as wide around as the state of Arizona." He shook his head. "Blew my mind. Still does. Anyway, he tossed me one of his magazines with an article about Mars. I read the issue of *Astronomy* cover to cover."

"And now you're hooked on stars?"

"Stars, planets, spacecraft, primordial black holes... I know it seems out of character, but I needed a hobby. The more I learned about space, the more peaceful I was on Earth. Good timing too, because while I was fitted for the bionic legs, I was reading about the advancements in engineering and exploration in space. The human race is a mess, but there are some seriously brave and brilliant people on this planet."

"Sorry I gave you a hard time about it. I'm all for anything bringing you peace."

"And I knew every answer in the 'Astronomy' category when *Jeopardy* was on in an airport. People thought I was a genius." Scott pointed at the windshield and said, "Here's the lake." A small body of water appeared before them, and the rippling surface became more visible as the headlamps swept over the lake. Brenner turned left when the road split in two. "But enough about my new hobby. I promised to tell you about my new legs before we got to the schoolhouse."

"You don't have to tell us right now," Ivy said. "Or ever, really."

"No, I want to. It won't take long, and you should know. I lost one and a half legs to an IED. My left leg is gone from the kneecap down, and my right leg is gone from the mid-thigh down. During recovery, I met a scientist in England who develops bionic limbs. Her company consulted on military prosthetics, and I was lucky enough to get a new pair of legs. The wiring is connected to my nervous system, so I can control my legs with my brain, like I used to do."

"Bionic limbs for the military?" Lauren asked. Scott nodded, and she said, "Amazing."

"Hey, did your Air Force roomie get a super arm?" asked Brenner.

"He did! I'm not allowed to talk about it, but it's beyond badass."

After the truck made its way around the left bank of the lake, the road straightened, and Brenner saw the second gate. Pointing to it, he asked Scott, "This is how we get out?"

"Yep." Brenner stopped the truck so Scott could get out. "I promise to not slam it shut."

"How thoughtful." Brenner rolled his eyes. "Now hurry up."

"You want me to hurry? Watch this."

CHAPTER ELEVEN

Lauren

FTER SETTING A PERSONAL RECORD FOR QUICKLY OPENING and closing a gate, Scott called Wyatt Underwood to thank him for letting them use his farm's shortcut. He mentioned spotting a whitetail buck on the property but left the close encounter out of his recap. Lauren was grateful their exit was uneventful compared to their arrival. She'd been deeply touched when Scott shared how he came to be a double amputee and accidental astronomer. She was processing all the surprises, and she knew this would forever be the most extraordinary shortcut of her life.

Lauren leaned a bit to the right and squinted at the landscape through the windshield. She knew where they were, and she sent up a prayer as the road curved toward the right. "It'll be around this corner," she said. A tall chain-link fence came into view, separating the street from an unkempt plot of land. Lauren scanned the area, seeing overgrown weeds, a few trees, and one abandoned school-house. "It's still there!"

"It's still standing!" Ivy clapped. "You are winning this contest, Lauren!"

Brenner pulled over at an angle so his headlights would shine on the front of the schoolhouse. They all got out of the truck and looked at the building through the chain-link fence. Their bodies blocked the light coming from the truck, and their collective shadow darkened the one-story building. Scott, Ivy, and Brenner stepped away from the headlights to allow the light through. Lauren sat on the grass below the lights and lifted her phone against the chain-link fence, trying to frame the shot through a diamond-shaped chain link. She took a few pictures but wasn't happy with the images.

"Want me to turn on the brights?" Lauren nodded, and Brenner reached in his truck and switched on the high beams. The schoolhouse was drenched with LED lighting, making it difficult to look at the building.

Scott shielded his eyes. "Damn, B."

Lauren knew her photo would be washed out, but she took it anyway. As expected, the front of the structure was obscured by light. "Low beams it is," she said to Brenner. "But it was a great idea."

After Brenner turned off the high beams, Lauren had to blink away the white spots bouncing before her eyes.

"I'll have to get closer," she said. "Use the truck for light, but take the photo from the side."

"I'll bring these in case." Brenner reached into the truck and grabbed the flashlights and headlamps they had used for the dumpster dive. "Sully, you see any security?" he asked before he locked his truck.

"Negative." Scott said, "Not even barbed wire. It's almost too easy."

It hadn't occurred to Lauren to scan the area for security. "There is one filthy 'No Trespassing' sign." Brenner tossed the equipment over the fence. As the flashlights and headlamps crossed the top, Lauren looked at him. "I'd love help getting over the fence, but all of us don't need to trespass for me to take a picture."

"Ivy wasn't kidding when she called it a death trap." Brenner pointed to the left corner of the battered roof. "It won't take much for those shingles to give up the fight. A strong wind would do it. Or rodents."

"Rodents?" It hadn't occurred to Lauren to scan the area for animals either. "In that case, I'd love backup. Thank you."

"It's not the safest location, so let's be quick about it." He kneeled down, linked his fingers and turned his palms up, making a step for Lauren. "Ladies first. We'll give you a boost and follow behind."

Scott also knelt down. As Ivy put one shoe in his palms, she said, "You can leap this fence in a single bound, right?"

"Of course, but in keeping with the spirit of the mission, I'll do it the old-school way." He lifted Ivy up, and she placed her other foot in an opening in the chain link. "Old school. Get it?"

"Good Lord, your jokes need work."

"Don't act like you don't love my jokes, Ivy. I saw you smile."

"You saw me grimace."

"If you say so, woman."

"Seriously, stick to the celestial metaphors." She raised her foot to a hole in the fence. "Do not look up my dress."

"I'm closing my eyes until you're on the other side, Scout's honor." He closed his eyes and reached for Ivy's calf with one hand. He gave it a gentle squeeze. "You good?"

"I'm great." Ivy made her way up and over the

nine-foot fence. After she swung her second leg to the other side, Ivy looked down at Scott. His eyes were shut, and his head turned to the side, but his arms were stretched out directly above him in the area Ivy had been climbing. "I made it halfway. You can open your eyes now."

Lauren waited until Ivy was on the other side of the fence before she began climbing. After she reached the ground on the other side, Brenner efficiently followed her over and together they walked to the patch of weeds where his flashlights had landed. Brenner picked up the headlamp and handed it to Lauren. "You should use this one," he said. "It gives off good light, and it'll keep your hands free for taking pictures."

"Good thinking. I'm going to need all the light I can get to take a decent photo."

They heard laughing behind them and turned. Scott was already on the ground on their side, and Ivy was four feet from the bottom. He grabbed her waist with both hands and lifted her off the fence. "Hey! I can make it."

"I know." Scott slowly lowered her to the grass. "But we're in a hurry, and it was a great excuse to get my hands on you."

"These two," Brenner said with a sigh. "We'll be lucky if they wait until after the contest to elope in Vegas."

"If Ivy wasn't smitten before his star analogy, she is now."

Lauren's phone sounded out with a new text alert. She lifted it from her back pocket and showed Brenner the message.

Amy: Everybody okay?

She kept her phone where they both could see the screen, silently inviting Brenner to read along.

Lauren: Doing great. About to take an old school photo.

Amy: ?

Amy: Like with 35 mm film?

Lauren: No—lol—it's the hashtag I'm on.

Lauren: #OldSchool

Amy: Oh! Right! Go take your picture.

Amy: Ivy okay?

Lauren raised her phone to take a photo of Scott and Ivy leaning against the fence and sent it to Amy.

Lauren: ^ You tell me.

Amy: Oh snap. Ivy's a happy girl.

Lauren and Brenner laughed at Amy's comment.

Amy: What about you? You making eyes with the #hottie?

Lauren immediately lowered her phone. "Of course she did." She couldn't bring herself to look at Brenner. "I must be breaking a world record for most embarrassing moments in a single night."

"Please don't be embarrassed. I look forward to making eyes with you when we don't have to babysit the kids or win a contest." Brenner lifted Lauren's chin so she'd look at him. "I was beyond embarrassed when the gate slammed and I tore off in the truck. I scared you and Ivy, and I should have done a better job of apologizing."

"The noise scared everyone. Even the damn deer panicked."

"I know it looked erratic, but in my mind, I was keeping you safe. You never drive in a straight line when it's raining mortar fire…in a war zone on the other side of the planet." Brenner shook his head. "But I was driving my own truck through a pumpkin farm in North Carolina."

"You have nothing to be embarrassed about, Brenner."

"Then neither do you, okay?"

119

Amy: Where'd you go?

Amy: Still alive?

Brenner put his arm around Lauren's shoulder. "Let's send Amy a picture of us and show her how the cool kids do it."

Lauren swapped the camera to the selfie setting and tried to get them both in the frame. "You're a tall one."

"Here, let me take it. I've got long arms." Brenner raised the phone up to take the shot. The arm resting on Lauren's shoulder slid down her arm as he cuddled in close for a picture. "Say 'hashtags!'"

"Hashtags!" Lauren laughed, and Brenner handed her phone back. "Tell her I say hi."

Standing so close to Brenner was distracting. Lauren could send a selfie in her sleep, but she fumbled through the text. Probably because he still had his arm around her.

A cough made Lauren and Brenner look up. Ivy was pretending to be put out but couldn't keep the grin off her face. Scott's incredulous look seemed genuine. He pointed at Brenner and asked, "Did you take a selfie, soldier?"

"Yeah, so? She's sending Amy proof of life."

"With a selfie." Scott moved his fingertips to his temples and gave the international signal for "mind-blown."

"What's your problem with me taking a selfie with Lauren?"

"There's no problem. First time for everything." Scott scratched his jaw. "Now I understand my conversation about interstellar clouds coming as a shock."

"Not even close to the same thing, Sully." Brenner handed Scott and Ivy each a flashlight. "Time to focus, kids. Lauren's going to tell us where to point these so she can get a decent picture."

They walked as a group toward the schoolhouse entrance, aiming the flashlights on the ground before their feet. Ivy made her way to Lauren and tucked her arm in her friend's elbow. With a slight tug on Lauren's arm, Ivy brought them to a stop, and the men continued walking.

Ivy could only manage a pseudo whisper. "What in the actual what-what just happened?"

"Shh!" Lauren looked ahead to where Brenner and Scott were shining their flashlights on the schoolhouse. "We bonded over embarrassing moments. He wants to hang out sometime minus the hashtags and friends."

"I'm too excited to be even a little bit offended." With another tug, they resumed their walk to the front of the schoolhouse.

"So, what are you thinking?" asked Brenner.

Lauren took in the dilapidated building. "If we all shine a light on a part of it, it may help with the shadows from the truck's lights. Ivy, you get the steps and porch."

"You mean the heap of busted bricks and rotten wood?"

"Yes, ma'am. Brenner, you get the front door and windows."

"Sure thing." His flashlight swept over the tall weeds and up the crumbled steps before it settled on the weathered exterior wall. The timber frame was warped from moisture and gouged at the edges from insects. Overlapping pieces of plywood barred entry through the school's only door. There was no glass remaining in the window frames, leaving the interior exposed to the elements. Through the openings, Brenner's flashlight illuminated rotten timber, broken plaster, and the exhaust pipe for a wood-burning stove.

"Scott, will your light reach the bell tower?"

"It's adjustable, so it should." Scott changed the beam from a floodlight to a spotlight, with the light focused on the wooden belfry. The bell was missing, as were most of the slats that would have secured the square structure to the A-frame roof.

"If bats come out of there, I'll need your ten grand for therapy." Ivy looked at Lauren. "I'm not kidding."

"Move your light a little to the left, and it's a deal." Lauren held her phone and framed the shot. "There! Perfect."

"Brenner, can you widen your beam too?"

"Yep."

"Try to reach the boards with red paint."

Brenner twisted his flashlight until the broad beam revealed the edges of the exterior wall.

"Yes!" Lauren took her time zooming in and out on her phone's screen. When she was happy with the lighting and composition, she took several pictures. Flipping through them, she said, "I got some great shots!"

A gust of wind lifted roof shingles and the loud, distinctive hoot of a barred owl carried across the countryside. The schoolhouse emitted a series of creaks and groans.

Ivy said, "Lauren, how about you text the Wizard from the other side of the fence?"

Lauren put her phone in her back pocket. "Good idea."

More sounds came from the building and they all ran to the fence. Scott helped Ivy get started, and with a boost from Brenner, Lauren was on her way. As if they were racing each other, the men scrambled up and over the fence.

"Man, this is fun," Scott said after they dropped to the ground. He gave Brenner a high five. "What number hashtag was this?"

"Seven," Lauren answered as she climbed over the top of the fence.

"Your Wizard will love it." Brenner hugged Lauren when she joined him on the other side. "I dare anyone to find a better old school."

"Thanks to my lighting crew, the pictures turned out great." She hugged him back before reaching for her phone. Lauren scrolled through her gallery, selected her favorite image, and texted the Wizard. "Photo sent." She slid the phone into her back pocket, and moments later they all heard her text alert. "Bet it's Amy," she said.

Brenner was standing next to her and saw the screen at the same time Lauren did. "It's from the Wizard."

"Already?" Ivy was still clinging to the fence. "But you sent it five seconds ago." Like he did on the other side, Scott plucked Ivy off the chain links and set her softly on the ground. Instead of fussing with him for "helping," she rushed to Lauren's side. "It's too fast. Is it bad news?"

"Nope! Our old school was accepted, and look at number eight!"

Ivy read the text aloud.

Challenge 8 of 12: #Anchor
Time Remaining: 5 hours and 37 minutes

"Awesome!" Lauren and Ivy hugged as Scott and Brenner looked on in confusion. "Yes! We finally got an easy one!"

CHAPTER TWELVE

Brenner

"**E**ASY?" BRENNER ASSUMED HE'D MISHEARD IVY. "YOU said 'anchor,' right?"

Both women nodded and smiled.

Scott opened his arms wide. "There's a stockpile of anchors way out here in God's country?"

"She needs one anchor, and it's closer than you think." Ivy turned Lauren's body toward the truck so her back was to Scott and Brenner. "You two stand by the fence."

Ivy raised the hem of Lauren's shirt, and Brenner asked, "What's happening right now?"

"Wait!" Lauren stopped Ivy's hand with her own. "It won't get me disqualified, right?"

"Is 'tattoo' on the list of no-nos?"

"You have a tattoo? Of an anchor?" Brenner clicked his flashlight on and aimed it at Lauren's back. "Lighting crew reporting for duty."

Lauren pointed at the headlights shining on her body. With a flirty smile over her shoulder, she said, "Got plenty of light, but thanks."

Ivy raised an eyebrow. "If you want to help, look up

the contest rules while she takes a picture."

"I read the rules a thousand times." Lauren unbuttoned and unzipped her jeans. "I don't remember anything about tattoos."

"Better safe than sorry," Ivy said. "Don't want to get this far and blow it. If we need real anchors, we'll haul ass to the fish camp in Fort Mill."

"Genius!"

Brenner listened to Lauren and Ivy and recalled his confusion in Barkley's Pub. Standing on the periphery of an unusual conversation, disoriented by the discussion. He must have been gawking because Scott closed his slack jaw with a finger.

Snapping the fingers on his other hand, Scott said, "I can employ knife hands and a drill sergeant tirade if I have to."

"I'm good." Brenner cleared his throat. "Not sure how many more surprises I can take tonight."

"Best. Night. Ever." Scott slapped him on the shoulder. "And to think we would've missed it if your hotness wasn't out in the wild." He pointed to Brenner's phone. "Find those rules. The lady needs help."

Brenner opened the app and heard Ivy say, "I cannot get my mind around #OldSchool getting approved so fast. It's like the Wizard was sitting around waiting for a photo."

"I'm so glad we drove out here." Lauren put her camera on selfie mode and lined up her shot. "And this one could be another quick yes."

"I know! It's so exciting!" Ivy looked over Lauren's shoulder to talk to Brenner. "What do the rules say?"

Brenner repeated the section Anthony had read in Barkley's Pub. "'Participants will be removed from the

Hashtag Hunt if photos are manipulated, staged, or affected by the photographer in any way. Any posed or constructed image submitted as a "found moment" is cause for immediate disqualification. Do not submit the following: a picture of another photograph, screenshots, or any photo altered by editing software, camera filters, or third-party apps. Any accepted entry, the picture and/or the subject(s) in it, may not be resubmitted for another challenge during the course of the contest.'"

"Tattoo is not mentioned," Scott said. "You should be alright."

Ivy asked, "What was the part about a picture of a picture?"

Brenner repeated, "A picture of another photograph is not allowed."

"A tattoo isn't a photograph, and it's as real as it gets." Ivy jumped up and down. "Take it! If the Wizard doesn't accept the photo, we'll appeal."

Facing the headlamps, Lauren set the timer and began the countdown. After the picture had been captured, Lauren studied the image. She nodded and handed the phone to Ivy. While she was straightening her clothes, Ivy said, "I take it all back. I love this tattoo."

"Not a fan of tats, Ivy?" Scott took a few steps toward them but abruptly stopped. "Lauren, you decent?"

"I am now." She reclaimed her phone from Ivy. After a few taps of her thumb, Lauren returned her phone to her back pocket. "Ivy's not big on ink or any piercings beyond earrings."

"Is that right?" Scott leaned one hip against Brenner's truck. "Well, you're in luck. I used to have Captain America's shield on my right calf." Scott smiled and said, "I thought about putting it on my shoulder after my surgeries, but getting the same tattoo twice doesn't sit well."

Ivy stepped close to him and wrapped her arms around his waist. "You're more Iron Man these days anyway."

Scott laughed and pulled her in for a hug. "How about an ivy leaf right over my heart?" He nuzzled the top of her head. "Too soon?"

"Way, way too soon." She looked up at him and smiled. "And it's the kiss of death for all relationships. We'd break up five minutes after you got it. There are plenty of other ways to show you're into me."

"A compromise: on our lampshade-shopping date, we get an ivy plant for my place."

"You know ivy's a vine, right?" She hugged him tightly before stepping out of their embrace. "It's a stubborn, hearty plant that attaches itself with little hooks when it finds a warm, bright place." She made little hooks with her fingers and snagged them on his shirt.

Scott covered them with his hands. "You are what I need in my life, Ivy... Wait. What's your full name?"

"Ivy Grace Prescott."

"Ivy Grace." Scott wrapped his arms around her. "I'm Scott Cooper Sullivan. So nice to meet you."

Lauren and Brenner looked away when their friends kissed for the second time. "We're losing them," she joked.

"Let them have a minute until the next hashtag comes in." He turned his body so they faced each other. "So, all this time you've been hiding a tattoo." Brenner shook his head. "It's always the quiet ones."

Lauren laughed. "Would you like to see it?" Brenner's eyes widened before they glanced at her hip. She held up her phone. "I meant would you like to see a picture of my tattoo?"

His voice was unusually raspy when he answered. "Yes, please." She pulled up the photo and handed him her phone.

Brenner had never seen a tattoo like Lauren's. No heavy lines, only delicate swathes and spatters of blues and greens spreading across her hip in a surprising watercolor effect. The anchor itself was not inked into her skin because it took its shape from the negative space among the blended watercolors. "It's incredible."

"Thank you. It took a year to save up for an artist known for this technique." Lauren looked at the photo with Brenner. "I love it."

"Why hide something so beautiful on your hip?"

"One: it's easily concealed. Two: the colors last if they're not exposed to sunlight." Brenner nodded. "And three: it's something special, so only special people can see it."

"Like the Wizard," Brenner joked. "And me."

"Well, technically you both saw a picture of my tattoo, so…" She winked at him.

"It's still an honor. Thanks for trusting me with your secrets." Brenner took her hand. "So, why an anchor?"

"It signifies a safe passage through a bumpy life." She rubbed her left hip. "Compared to a boat, it's so small, but it's more than enough to do the job. It goes where I go. Cast it out when I want to be still or feel secure. It works against the current so I'm not swept away."

"Very cool." Brenner stood up straight and raised the front of his Henley precisely high enough to show Lauren the tattoo he had inked over his rib cage. Unlike Lauren's delicate ebb and flow of the watercolor technique, his symbol was a bold blackwork design. Heavily outlined geometric shapes formed sturdy feathers, a hooked beak, and two vigilant eyes. Intricate dotwork within the shapes gave the art dimension, and the end result was a pen and ink illustration.

Lauren reached out to touch the tattoo but stopped before her fingers grazed Brenner's skin. She lowered her hand. "It's awesome."

"Thanks." He lowered his shirt and relished Lauren's gaze following the fabric's path down his torso.

When she finally met his eyes, she blushed and asked, "Lots of Army symbols. Why the eagle?"

"I've always liked eagles, even before I enlisted. I studied them for a school project, and as creatures go, they're badass." Brenner didn't want to bore her with fun facts about eagles, so he only mentioned two. "They fly higher than any other bird, and they can go up to one hundred miles per hour when they dive for prey."

"One hundred miles an hour?"

Brenner nodded and because he couldn't help himself, he added, "They even fly above a storm and stay dry while every other type of bird seeks shelter."

"They don't do anything halfway, huh?" Lauren laughed.

"Nope." Brenner crossed his arms.

Lauren nodded toward the truck. "Let's make our way back to town and find a gas station. I'll fill up your tank and get some snacks."

"Yes, except for the part where you buy my gas and Slim Jims."

Lauren jerked away from Brenner with a gasp. "Oh, thank God."

"What did I miss?"

"I was beginning to think you were perfect."

"Perfect?" Brenner laughed. "You were in the truck back there, right?" When Lauren nodded, he lifted his hands and asked, "And what'd I do now?"

"You eat Slim Jims."

"What's wrong with Slim Jims?" Brenner could take or leave the dried sausage snack but wanted more of this playful side of Lauren. "Are you a vegetarian?"

"Lord, no. Not even a little bit."

"Is eating Slim Jims a deal-breaker?"

Lauren met his eyes. "I'll make an exception for you."

"Glad to hear it."

"There are worse things, and honestly, it's a relief to know something's wrong with you."

"And what about you? What's wrong with you?" Brenner asked.

"How much time you got?"

At that moment, Brenner knew seeing Lauren smile would never get old. "You have until we reach the gas station to mention something I won't find attractive." Brenner headed toward the truck. Over his shoulder, he said, "Good luck with that. Time starts now."

Scott and Ivy had been taking selfies by the tailgate. When Brenner and Lauren approached the truck, Scott asked, "So what's the plan?"

"Get to a gas station. We'll top off the truck and get some snacks while we wait for the next hashtag. Charge our phones." Brenner walked past his door to open Lauren's. "Good luck finding something I don't like about you."

Before Lauren got in the backseat, she faced Brenner.

"I hate horror movies."

"So do I."

Her shoulders sank. "But guys love scary movies."

Brenner shrugged. "Not all guys. What else you got?"

Lauren stared at him and smiled. "I'll think of something." She got in the truck, and before he shut her door, she said, "I'm far from perfect."

"Nobody's perfect. But you are authentic, and being real trumps being perfect. All. Day." He gently shut her door and opened his own.

When Scott got in the passenger seat, he looked at Brenner and said, "Damn, son."

"What?" Brenner started the truck. "It's not as romantic as gas exploding in outer space, but I meant it all the same." He met Lauren's eyes in the rearview mirror and smiled, hoping she liked his dimples.

Lauren looked at Ivy and said, "Help me convince Brenner I have a fault."

Brenner chuckled to himself at the disbelief in Ivy's voice when she asked, "What? Why?"

"I eat Slim Jims," Brenner said.

"I can live with the Slim Jims." Lauren said over Ivy's gasp and dramatic interpretation of clutching an imaginary strand of pearls. "Only fair I tell him something about me he won't like."

"I don't get this game you're playing." Ivy looked out her window. "You both need to work on your flirting skills."

Brenner looked over his right shoulder to talk to Lauren. "There's not much you can say that'll stop me from asking you out tomorrow."

"Why don't you ask her out right now?" Scott asked.

Brenner cut his eyes to the passenger seat. "Because I'm not asking when she's sitting behind me in my truck in the middle of her contest."

"Oh! I know!" Lauren leaned forward in her seat. "Here's something you won't like about me."

Brenner said, "Let's hear it."

"I hate the New England Patriots."

Brenner gasped, and Scott slammed his hands on the dashboard and turned in his seat to face Lauren. "You. Hate. The. Pats?"

"I do, and I love to hate them. Especially Shady Brady."

"B, you need to lock this down." Scott scratched his chin. "Maybe pull over and propose right here."

Brenner nodded. "Lauren, you may never get rid of me."

"Because I hate the Pats?"

"You had me at 'Shady Brady,' beautiful."

By the time he parked beside a gas pump, Lauren still hadn't heard from the Wizard. Scott and Ivy entered the convenience store for coffee and carbohydrates. After Lauren texted Amy with an update, she got out of the truck to stand by Brenner. He began the process of filling up his tank and grew frustrated with the screen's prompts.

"When did getting gas become a round of Twenty Questions? Do I have a rewards club card? Do I want a car wash? Debit or credit?" He jabbed his finger against the worn-out buttons before he entered his zip code and was allowed to make his gas selection. "Enough already."

"It is obnoxious." Lauren leaned against her door

while Brenner put the fuel nozzle in his gas tank. "And just when you think you can get on with your life, it waits til the very end to ask if you want a receipt."

"Way too much interaction with a gas pump. It's enough to make me throw cash on the counter next time." Once the gas started flowing, he shook his head. "Anyway, I should warn you that Sully's probably buying me Slim Jims. Will you mind if I eat them in front of you?"

"Of course not."

"Does the probability of us kissing after the contest go down if I eat them?" When Lauren looked away as if she was considering his question, Brenner thought he'd pushed too far.

"Well, if I win this contest, I'm kissing you regardless of your Slim Jim breath." She returned her gaze to him. "But in case I don't win…you should kiss me now."

"Alright, you asked for it." Brenner locked the lever in the handle to keep the gas flowing and stepped over the thick black hose. Her back was against the truck, and he stepped closer to her. Keeping his body a respectable distance from hers, he framed her face with his hands and leaned in. Brenner looked in her eyes and smiled. "I wish I'd met you sooner."

"You were right on time tonight."

"I'd forgotten what it was like to look forward to something. The past few years, I've felt an obligation, dread, fear, sadness, confusion. Guilt."

"And what are you feeling now?"

"Joy. Excitement. Wonder." The first kiss was a soft, brief one. "Hope." The kisses that followed were tender and promising. And slightly restrained, as if they minded their manners. The kisses delivered a mutual, unspoken message of wanting more when time allowed for passion to play a part in their affection. When they heard her phone's text alert, they reluctantly pulled out of the moment. Brenner ended the last kiss the same way he'd started the first one: with eye contact and a smile.

CHAPTER THIRTEEN

Lauren

L AUREN KNEW SHE SHOULD BE CHECKING HER PHONE, BUT savoring this stolen moment was also essential. Kissing Brenner in a gas station was every bit as unexpected as the hashtags she'd been hunting. The contest was going well, and the attraction was apparently mutual. When she stole glances at him, he was already staring. Despite the urgency of the competition, she wanted this feeling to linger. Lauren's bliss bubble popped when the gas pump cut off with a loud click.

Brenner stepped back over the hose to return it to the pump. As Scott and Ivy exited the convenience store, he pointed at them and said, "We'll be as wrapped up as those two if we don't focus." With a wink, he added, "Check your messages."

"Right." Lauren got the phone out of sleep mode and was greeted to the words "Challenge 9 of 12…" She bounced up and down a few times but froze on the spot once she read the whole text.

Challenge 9 of 12: #Helicopter

Time Remaining: 4 hours and 57 minutes

"Is it from the Wizard?" Brenner replaced the gas cap and closed the hatch.

"She got a text?" Ivy squealed and hustled to the truck while holding two to-go cups of coffee. "What's it say?"

"Helicopter."

Ivy passed the coffees to Brenner and stood next to Lauren to see the screen for herself.

"What, like a real helicopter?"

Scott rounded the truck and lowered the tailgate. "Can't be sitting in the toy aisle at the twenty-four-hour Walmart, right?" He set down the bag of snacks and fished out a bag of Fritos. "Your Wizard wants the real deal?"

Brenner joined Scott behind his truck and gestured toward the tailgate with one of the coffees. "Ladies, have a seat." Brenner stepped back so Lauren could lift herself on the metal ledge. He glanced around and said, "We're not in anyone's way. Let's talk it out."

Scott lifted Ivy and placed her next to Lauren on the tailgate. Ivy opened her mouth to speak, and Scott gently pressed his finger against her lips. "I know. My alpha is showing." He stepped back when Brenner handed Ivy her coffee. "Any chance 'caveman tendencies' is on your list of turn-ons?"

Ivy peeled the lid off the Styrofoam cup and watched the steam billow. "No comment."

Lauren couldn't help but laugh. She was well acquainted with Ivy's extensive alpha romance Kindle collection. The hero of the story varied from retired military, wealthy CEOs with eight-pack abs, athletes, cowboys, firemen, and rock stars. Ivy recently shared she was on a historical kick, with disgraced dukes, Highland lairds, and rogue pirates. Lauren was also a fan of romance novels and was currently rereading one of her favorites about a bootlegger's sassy daughter and a sexy mobster in Prohibition-era Detroit. Wanting to get back on track, she looked at Brenner and said, "We need a helicopter."

Brenner began peeling apart the Slim Jim's wrapper. "We've got helicopters on base, but it's a two-and-a-half-hour drive."

"I don't have that kind of time." Lauren tapped her phone against her forehead. "Think. Where would a city have a helicopter?"

Ivy answered, "News stations. Police stations."

Scott added. "Private airstrips have hangars for personal use."

"Know anyone who has a helicopter for personal use?" joked Brenner.

"I don't know anyone who…" Lauren's voice trailed off before returning with an excited "Oh!" She scrolled through the contacts on her phone, regretting she hadn't thought of Katie sooner.

Ivy leaned over and saw who Lauren was calling. "Yes! Genius!" Ivy crossed her fingers right before Lauren closed her eyes and raised the phone to her ear. It took two rings for her friend to answer.

"Go ahead, caller. You're on the air."

Lauren's eyes popped open. "Katie! Thank you for picking up. I swear you're the only one who does anymore."

"What's up, girl?"

Ivy clapped and leaned into the phone's speaker. "Hi, Katie! It's Ivy."

"You two okay?" The voice coming from the phone

changed from jovial to concerned.

"Oh, yes. Everything's okay. I know it's after midnight, but I need a favor. Huh?" Lauren raised her eyebrows and turned her head toward Ivy. "Yes, for the hashtag contest. How did you know?" She relayed Katie's answer to Ivy. "Jess posted the group picture on Facebook." Returning to her phone conversation, Lauren said, "So, for the contest, I need to take a picture of a helicopter…and I'm hoping you can help me." Lauren smiled at Brenner. "You're on duty now?" Lauren grabbed Ivy's hand. "You can? Oh, thank you! We're on our way. I'll text you when we get there. Thanks again! Bye."

Ivy and Lauren scrambled off the tailgate. Scott and Brenner got the snacks, waters, and coffees and closed the tailgate.

"So who's Katie?" Scott asked.

"She's only the Paramedic of the Year, thank you very much." Lauren was so proud of her friend. "She works on the life flight helicopter!"

When everyone was in the truck, Brenner started the engine and asked, "So where we headed?"

Lauren buckled her seat belt and said, "CMC Main."

"What's that?"

"A hospital." Scott pointed to the left. "We need to head back toward the college. It's only five minutes away from where we parked for the dumpster dive."

Ivy laughed. "Man, it feels like the dumpster challenge was forever ago."

Scott looked in the backseat and winked at Ivy. "Well, a lot's happened since I scored a sweet new lamp."

Ivy reached over and squeezed Lauren's hand. "I am so happy for you!"

Scott played navigator as Brenner made his way to the hospital. When they were at a red light, Brenner asked Lauren, "Still in second place, hotshot?"

"I can't believe I didn't check after the Wizard's text! Hang on!" Lauren opened the app and clicked on the leaderboard. Her gasp resonated through the cab.

"You take the lead?" Ivy shouted.

Lauren nodded, and the truck erupted in cheers. Brenner honked his horn three times, and Ivy launched herself at Lauren for a tackle hug. "First place!" Lauren started to shake and blinked back her tears. In her ear, Ivy whispered, "You are amazing. You deserve this. You deserve much more, but it's a start."

"Oh my God, my heart's racing." Lauren hugged Ivy back. "Thanks for canceling your date."

"Don't thank me." Ivy nodded toward the passenger seat. "It was for purely selfish reasons. I could've missed all the excitement."

"I'd be lost without you."

"Hospital's up ahead." Scott directed Brenner through two left turns and then pointed out the parking deck.

"Visitors' lot!" Lauren reached forward and grabbed Brenner's shoulder. "My car's still parked at Regents!"

Ivy said, "It's close by. We'll swing by after you get the helicopter photo."

Lauren unbuckled her seat belt as Brenner pulled into a parking space. "I can't believe I forgot about my car."

"Well, you've had a lot on your mind." Ivy wiggled her eyebrows. "Now, let's knock out another hashtag."

Lauren texted Katie as they walked toward the hospital.

Lauren: We're here. Meet in the lobby?

Katie: Yes. Give me a few minutes to get there.

Katie: Checking on a patient.

Lauren: Take your time.

Katie: See you soon!

As they walked through the hospital's sliding glass doors and into the lobby, Lauren said, "Katie will meet us here in a few minutes."

Ivy pointed to the sign for the restrooms. "Let's take advantage of well-lit, clean facilities."

Scott's gaze followed Ivy's finger. "Good idea."

The group split in two as they walked into the men's and women's bathrooms. When she entered an empty stall, Lauren recalled sending Brenner's #HitW photo while hiding from Jess. She couldn't contain her laugh.

"You okay, Lauren?" The concern in Ivy's voice made her laugh harder.

"Thinking about how far I've come since I texted you from the ladies' room at Barkley's."

"Oh?" Ivy's voice took a teasing tone. "And just how far have you come exactly?"

"Brenner kissed me."

"What?"

"I kissed him back."

Lauren heard frantic shuffling and the deafening roar of Ivy's toilet flushing. "When? Where? You better pee fast and get your sneaky ass out here!" Lauren heard Ivy gasp. "Oh, I'm sorry, ma'am. I didn't know there were kids in here."

"It's totally okay," said a soft, tired voice. "They've heard worse from me, I promise."

When she was ready, Lauren opened the door to her stall. She saw a very young child strapped in a stroller. He was staring at Ivy. His mother was laying a baby on the diaper change station. Ivy was red-faced, staring at her hands as she washed them. Lauren joined her at the sinks, and they both started laughing.

"I feel awful," Ivy muttered.

"Don't," said the woman changing a diaper. "You two actually made me smile on what has been an awful day smothered and covered in mom guilt. These little guys are hanging out in a hospital instead of asleep at home. You can't predict where the day will take you." She smiled at the baby as she finished dressing him. "But sometimes days have excellent surprises, like the first kiss with a new guy." She arranged the infant in the sling wrap around her torso and got behind the stroller. Ivy rushed to open the door for the woman. "Thank you," she said. Before she walked through the door, she said, "Eventually, other things become more important, but it is thrilling when your priority is spending time together…kissing." She winked at Lauren and pushed the stroller out of the bathroom.

Ivy let the door close behind the mother. "Only a hunch, but spending time together kissing is probably why she has Irish twins."

Lauren laughed and dried her hands. "I'll tell you all about kissing Brenner when we have time. Katie's expecting us." Before they reached the door, Lauren grabbed Ivy's arm to stop her. "Spoiler alert: it was the best first kiss of my life. By far."

"That's what I'm talking about." Ivy smacked Lauren on the rear end. "Now let's finish this thing so we all can get back to kissing." She rolled her eyes and opened the door. "You know what I mean."

Lauren spotted Katie standing at the information desk, chatting with hospital staff and a policewoman. Katie's black flight suit had teal stripes and reflective strips down the sleeves, and zippers scattered across her arms, legs, and chest. Specialized pockets held the tools of her trade. Her hospital ID hung from her shoulder, and a radio was clipped to her belt. When Katie saw Lauren, she pointed her out and said, "Here she is! Lauren Daniels! Holding down first place in whatever crazy contest thing she's doing tonight!" Katie welcomed Lauren and Ivy with hugs. "I downloaded the app. I was so pumped when you took the lead."

"Can you believe it? It's been a crazy night." Lauren was both grateful for and humbled by the encouragement. She'd nearly written the evening off when she'd been busted taking Brenner's picture. With Ivy's support and their new friends' assistance, she was in first place. "I've had so much help." Lauren took a step back to make introductions. "Katie, meet Brenner and Scott. They've been with us since Barkley's."

"It's so nice to meet you both." After she shook their hands, Katie said, "Jess mentioned two handsome heroes on Facebook." Katie made a point of studying both men before asking Lauren, "Which one was the hottie? From where I'm standing, they both qualify."

"I knew I liked you." Scott laughed and slapped Brenner on the shoulder. "She took his picture, but I can't thank you enough for asking."

"Well, it takes a hottie to know one, amiright?" Katie gestured for them to follow her. They passed the bank of elevators Lauren had assumed they'd be using. She turned a corner, and they all followed her down a hallway to another set of elevators. "This contest sounds tough, and I'm glad you've had help. Eye candy is always a nice bonus."

Lauren looked at Brenner and Scott and laughed. "It's been a great surprise. And I can't thank you enough for the helicopter hookup. I don't know what we'd be doing without you."

"I'm happy you called." Katie pressed the up button and said, "I know you're in a hurry, but I'll give you the nickel tour as we walk to the roof." The elevator doors opened, and Katie entered first. She scanned her hospital ID and pushed the button for the AirMedic Unit. "Hashtag, party of five. Going up."

Lauren gestured around the elevator as it began rising. "Are you sure it's okay for all of us to be here like this?"

"Totally fine! I wish more of my friends would come to visit me at work." The elevator ascended to the hospital's top floor. "You should have your photo in no time. One AirMedic is out getting fuel, but there's one prepped for flight on the helipad." She looked at her watch. "Your contest ends at five in the morning?"

"Yes." Lauren started to feel the pressure of racing the clock. "Don't remind me. There are three more to do after this one."

"Well, you've made it this far." Katie looked at Ivy, Scott, and Brenner. "And you've got a great team in your corner. You got this." When the elevator doors opened, Katie stepped out first and began her tour. "Welcome to the AirMedic Unit." In Lauren's opinion, it looked like the lobby of a bank, with a wall of offices on the right and two seating areas on the left. "Dispatch and the tower watch over our fleet of fixed-wing and rotor aircraft."

Ivy tapped Katie on her shoulder. "Your fleet of what?"

"Our planes and choppers, Ivy. Traumahawks. Relay rigs. Flying the amber lamps airways." She pointed to a collection of card games and puzzles on a bookshelf. "We have lots of time to kill between patients, but when we get a call, we race the Reaper."

"No doubt." Brenner cleared his throat. "Most of your calls about car accidents?"

Katie nodded. "All kinds of critical trauma, but we also transport patients between hospitals. Dispatch gets the call and informs the pilot about the flight plan and the crew about the patient."

"CENTCOM," Brenner and Scott said at the same time. When Lauren raised her eyebrows in confusion, Brenner added, "Central Command. Info in. Orders out."

"It's exactly like that." Katie continued walking down the hallway. "Most times, our patients are unconscious or in shock, so they don't remember their time with us. If they are alert, they're scared out of their minds, so we hold hands and encourage them while prepping them for the hospital. It's like an ambulance, only much smaller and going one hundred and forty miles per hour. In the air." Katie scanned her ID at the end of the hall and opened the double doors that led to the roof. "We have three helipads above this wing of the hospital. Pad Two has a helicopter ready for its close-up."

Lauren could not believe her luck. "I can't thank you enough, Katie. Really." Stepping out on the hospital roof at night was a bit disorienting. But as Katie said, a teal and white helicopter sat on a landing pad off to the right. "AIRMED" was boldly printed across the fuselage, and the hospital's logo and the EMS Star of Life were present, clearly identifying the helicopter as a rescue aircraft.

Katie's radio chirped, and she unclipped it from her belt. Into the speaker, she said, "AirMedic... You call, we haul." She listened to dispatch and said, "We have one prepped on Pad Two and one approaching Pad One." Katie pointed to a helicopter making its way to a landing pad on another section of the roof." To Lauren, she said, "If you have the time, you can get an action shot. We just got a call."

CHAPTER FOURTEEN

Brenner

ONCE KATIE UNCLIPPED HER RADIO FROM HER BELT, BRENNER excused himself from the group and leaned against the exterior wall. He wanted Lauren to get her photo without witnessing another evasive combat maneuver. The transition to civilian life had been more difficult than he'd anticipated.

Inhale for five seconds. Hold for three. Exhale for six. In for five. Hold. One, two, three. Out for six.

According to his counselor, Brenner's acute stress disorder was "a milder type of PTSD." He had common symptoms: insomnia, anxiety, heightened surveillance, and rapid response. He instinctively counted exits, found shade, and scanned the people around him for suspicious activity. He was up before dawn, inhaled his food, walked too fast, rolled his socks into balls, and often found himself reaching for the water bottle and combat knife he'd carried for years.

Katie took the call, and snippets of radio traffic by-passed the buzzing in his ears. "Heart harvested success-fully...match found...family notified...flight plan filed... Duke Children's Hospital...transplant team on alert...

pilot was refueling…approaching CMC now…yes, loading hot…requesting priority approach. Ten-four."

Brenner's attention turned to Lauren photographing the helicopter parked on its landing pad. He switched to a progressive relaxation technique he'd found to be effective. He tensed his toes and feet for a few seconds before relaxing them. And then did it again. He repeated the contract/release motions with his shins, knees, thighs, glutes, and chest. Brenner was flexing his shoulders when a blinding light appeared from the left. It illuminated the vacant helipad, and the whop, whop, whop of the rotor blades drowned out all sound on the roof deck. The double doors to Brenner's left flung open, and a woman in blue scrubs ran toward Katie. She was clutching a red and white cooler, and he could read the "HUMAN ORGAN FOR TRANSPLANT" label placed next to a biomedical hazard sticker.

Ivy, Scott, and Lauren left where they'd been standing and joined Brenner against the wall. Ivy pointed to the woman white-knuckling the cooler and shouted, "I can't believe we're watching this happen!"

Brenner took a deep breath and resumed his relaxation technique. He was contracting and releasing his shoulders when he felt Lauren's slim fingers skim the top of his hand. She rose to her tiptoes and spoke in his ear. "You okay?"

He bent down to answer her. "I will be." Brenner squeezed her palm before interlacing their fingers. "I'm slowing down my heart rate so I don't forget where I am. The hospital doesn't need any tactical defense demonstrations." He looked her in the eye and said, "If I try to move from this spot, slap me."

"You got it. We'll leave as soon as they take off." Lauren

kissed Brenner on the cheek. "I have tons of boring photos of the helicopter sitting over there, but I want to get this action shot if possible."

Brenner pointed to the scene playing out before them. "If I were the Wizard, I'd declare you the Hashtag Hunt champion outright for sending in a picture like this."

The pilot signaled the medical team, giving them permission to board. Katie leaned down to speak to another medic before running to her friends against the wall. "We're hauling it to Duke's," she shouted to Lauren. "Best of luck with the hashtags. Go get the ten grand, girl. We'll celebrate soon!"

"Sounds good. Thank you again!" Lauren let go of Brenner's hand long enough to hug Katie. "You are the very best. Always have been."

Katie hugged Lauren back before returning to her team near the helicopter. Over her shoulder, she yelled, "Be sure to get my good side!" Lauren lifted her cell phone, holding it horizontally with both hands. Katie was the last one to board. She closed the cabin door, and less than a minute later, the helicopter began to hover.

Lauren walked closer to the helipad and took several pictures of the vertical takeoff, not stopping until the AirMedic was entirely out of view. She thumbed through the photos on her way back and stopped short. "I shouldn't be so excited about this photo." Brenner loved the smile on Lauren's face as she tilted the screen toward Ivy.

"Send it! Quick!" Ivy squealed and said, "It looks like a commercial." She waved Brenner and Scott over. "Look at this!"

They joined the women and bent over Lauren's phone. Brenner shouldn't have been surprised the photo was so well lit. He'd noticed the rooftop's LED lighting, and nobody could miss the helicopter's high-intensity searchlight. The pilot's profile was visible through the cockpit window, and the lettering on the fuselage was in focus. "It's perfect."

"It's not too morbid?" Lauren asked.

Brenner looked from Lauren's phone to her face. He was surprised at the doubt he saw in her eyes. He and Scott both stood up straight and assured her it was a great photo.

"They are saving lives, woman!" Ivy pointed at the screen. "Hand delivering a heart to someone who needs it to live. It's a happy picture. It's hopeful, and it proves there's life after death."

Lauren nodded. "Right. Yeah, you're right." She tapped her thumb on the screen and texted the image to the Wizard.

"Attagirl." Ivy walked to the doors and opened one. "Let's go down to the lobby and wait for number ten." They backtracked down the hallway and approached the elevator. "Send it to Katie, too. She'll love it."

"Good call." Lauren texted Katie one more note of thanks and attached the photo. "Thanks to her, we saw two helicopters. I had options!"

The doors opened, and they entered the elevator. Scott pressed the button for the lobby and said, "This hashtag has been a bit surreal."

Brenner had been wondering what Sully thought of the medevac. He asked him, "Do you remember your transport?" Scott shook his head, and Brenner sighed in relief as the elevator began its slow slide to the first floor.

"All I remember is hearing 'dust-off inbound' and seeing medics bent over my legs. Then it all fades to black." Scott shrugged his shoulders. "The rest is a blur of hospital beds, pain, pain management, wheelchairs, physical therapy, prosthetics fittings—"

"Perks," Brenner interrupted. "Delta Force Edition perks."

Scott feigned a cough and huffed out the word "jealous."

"I am not jealous, Sully."

"Whatever, B. It's cool." Scott patted Brenner on the shoulder. "I'd be jealous too."

"I'm not jealous of your perks, brother. I am grateful you're still here." Brenner took advantage of the opportunity to say what had been on his mind since Sully leaped away from the deer. "You survived heavy mortar fire, multiple medevacs, and a double amputation."

"Like I said: jealous."

As the elevator slowed to a stop, Brenner said, "After all you've been through, you deserve classified bionic perks and a fun mission like this one tonight."

"Best night ever." Scott winked at Ivy as the doors opened. "No arguments here."

They filed out of the elevator and walked back the way they'd come with Katie. When they entered the hospital's spacious lobby, Lauren pointed to an empty sofa and said, "I need to sit down for a minute." She plopped herself in the middle of the couch and laid her phone face down on her right thigh. "I'm a little overwhelmed all of a sudden."

Brenner sat down next to Lauren, and she rested her head on his shoulder. "Take as much time as you need," he said, patting her knee with his hand. "It's been a long night." He'd assumed Lauren's adrenaline wouldn't crash until after the contest ended, but the impending deadline was stressful. Pile on an AirMedic dispatch and a brief account of Sully's recovery, and it was no wonder she'd hit a wall.

Scott sat down in an adjacent armchair and stretched out his legs. "It won't take long for the Wizard to approve your picture." Brenner noticed his friend's grimace when he said, "Rest up while you can."

"You must be exhausted," Ivy said as she sat down on the other side of Lauren. "You were at this for hours before we joined you."

"Yeah, I'm tired, but…" She raised her head from Brenner's shoulder and rubbed her eyes. "Watching Katie escort a human heart to a children's hospital puts things in perspective." She sighed and said, "With all that's going on in the world, so many awful headlines and heartbreaking news… I've been having fun chasing money all night."

"No, ma'am." Ivy got in Lauren's face and declared, "You've been chasing your dream all night. Big difference. This is about Paperback Vinyl. Your dream. Zero shame in having fun while goal digging."

"She's right." Brenner took hold of Lauren's palm and rubbed his thumb over the top of her hand. "Life is unpredictable, and you should make the most of the opportunities that come your way." Brenner knew he should take his own advice. He stayed under the radar these days, going through the motions of setting up an apartment and seeing his counselor. Brenner was living on his savings account, and the time would come when he'd need to decide what was next: another deployment, more college, new career. The only thing he was certain of was Sully's text had come at the perfect time. He squeezed Lauren's hand and said, "Luckily, some of life's surprises are amazing." Brenner warmed inside when she squeezed his hand back.

"This contest has been one surprise after another." Lauren tried to suppress a yawn, but she failed. "I'll rally if I get another hashtag."

"*When* you get another hashtag." Ivy was scrolling through her phone. "Your helicopter hashtag is epic."

"I hope the Wizard agrees with you. I need to get numbers ten, eleven, and twelve knocked out in the next—" Her phone signaled a new text, and she gasped. She turned it over in her lap, and Brenner, Ivy, and Scott sat up straight.

Brenner could see the text was from the Wizard, but realized it wasn't about the tenth hashtag after Lauren began reading the text out loud.

Photo Authentication Required

Greetings, @laurenburger.

Your #Helicopter photo is spectacular. I need you to verify it came from your phone's camera, or you'll be disqualified.

I've been enjoying your hashtags all night, and I'm 95% confident you witnessed this event... I'm hoping you took several pictures and sent me your favorite. Send me at least three other photos of the helicopter leaving the hospital.

You have thirty seconds. Time starts now.

"Holy crap." Lauren sat up straight, all signs of fatigue having vanished when she read the last three words.

"You didn't delete the photos, did you?" asked Ivy.

"No. Not yet." Lauren opened her phone's photo gallery and took a screenshot of the thumbnails. "Oh my God. My heart is pounding." She texted three consecutive images of the helicopter leaving the roof and the screenshot of her camera roll to the Wizard. "There. That was less than thirty seconds, right?"

"That was less than ten seconds," Brenner reassured her. "Thirty seconds is actually plenty of time to text someone three pictures."

"But nowhere near enough time to Photoshop three pictures." Scott tilted his head. "Pretty smart to put contestants on the spot to prove a photo is legit. You either have more photos like the one you sent her or you don't."

Lauren bounded up from the couch and began to pace in the lobby. Brenner wanted to comfort her, but he knew only the next hashtag would alleviate this stressful moment. He leaned back against the couch and watched her stare at her phone, willing a text to appear. She didn't have to wait long, and Brenner smiled when she breathlessly read the Wizard's words:

Photo Authentication Accepted
Challenge 10 of 12: #PayPhone
Time Remaining: 4 hours and 03 minutes

Lauren stopped pacing and stared at the screen. Brenner rose from his seat to stand next to her. "A pay phone, huh?" She stood so still, he thought she may be in shock. He put his arm around her and squeezed her shoulder. "If we can get two helicopters in five minutes, we can get one pay phone."

"I don't know." Lauren shook her head and looked at Brenner. "It might as well say 'hashtag: endangered species.' Oh, I feel sick."

Ivy looked around the lobby. "I bet hospitals are one of the few places that still have pay phones." Ivy stood up and said, "I'm going to the information desk to ask where we can find one."

Once Ivy left, Lauren rubbed her eyes and groaned. "A hundred bucks says there hasn't been a pay phone in this place in fifteen years."

"Minimum." Brenner tucked her into his side.

Scott chimed in. "But she gets an A for effort."

Ivy quickly returned. "The short answer is 'no,' and it came with some severe side-eye." She tucked her hair behind her ear and said, "The long answer involves how phone companies didn't make a profit from pay phones after cell phones and Skype became popular. They haven't had any in the hospital since the early 2000s."

"Not sure where we'll find one," Scott grunted. "Probably easier to get a tattoo of a pay phone."

"I'll do it." Ivy got her phone out of her purse and started searching online. "Tattoo parlors are open twenty-four seven, right?"

"Ivy." Lauren looked at her friend in disbelief. "If you're going to Google something right now, please Google 'where in the hell can we find a pay phone.'"

"Right. On it." Ivy's thumbs flew over her phone's screen. "It says the Henry Ford Museum of American Innovation… There's a whole exhibit going on over in Michigan." Ivy lowered her phone and looked at Lauren. "What about the Waffle House? Remember all the business cards for taxi cabs taped above the greasy pay phone by the exit?"

Brenner gave Lauren an incredulous look. "You took issue with my Slim Jims, yet you frequent the Waffle House?"

"I do not frequent the Waffle House." Lauren chuckled and then laughed so hard she drew attention from others in the lobby. She bent at the waist and belly-laughed until she cried.

Ivy was staring at her friend. "Lauren. You okay, boo?"

"Maybe. I don't know." Wiping the tears from her eyes,

she looked at Ivy. "I should ask you the same thing. Did you seriously Google tattoo parlors?"

"Offer still stands. It can be a little pay phone, right?"

"I would never, ever let you go through with it, but I love you for offering. And I already sent a picture of a tattoo, so it might count as a repeat entry." Lauren took a deep breath. "Sorry about getting a little high-maintenance back there. I'm good now." She held her hand out to Brenner. "Wanna drive around Charlotte and look for a pay phone?"

"You bet I do, beautiful." He took her hand and said, "Let's go."

CHAPTER FIFTEEN

Lauren

Lauren: Amy - you up?

Amy: New phone. Who dis?

Amy: Kidding.

Amy: Everybody okay?

Lauren: We're alive, but…

Ivy: We can't find a pay phone in this city.

Lauren: Do you have any ideas?

Amy: A pay phone?

Lauren: I've dropped to second place.

Amy: Does it have to work?

Lauren: Doubt it.

Amy: Okay. Where have you been?

Ivy: Might be easier to list where we haven't been.

Ivy: Googled 'pay phones near me' for over an hour.

Lauren: They're either inside a building with normal business hours or most of the pay phone parts are missing.

Ivy: We've tried the bus station, skating rinks, libraries…

Amy: Let me think.

Lauren: Gas stations, motels…

Amy: Promise me you're not in the shady parts of town at 3 a.m.

Ivy: We're safe. I'm with Scott in L's car and she is with Brenner in his truck.

Amy: So...not quite the end of the world.

Lauren: True, I could be in last place.

Amy: My new neighbors have a TARDIS in their backyard, but it's a free call.

Ivy: A what?

Lauren: They have a TARDIS?

Ivy: I repeat: a what?

Amy: Yes, girl. Life-size.

*Ivy: **Googles TARDIS***

Amy: Had a Doctor Who wedding.

Ivy: Okay... So it looks like a pay phone.

Amy: It only calls the closest police station.

Amy: For free.

Lauren laid her phone in her lap and sighed. "If only a TARDIS took coins."

"I don't know what that means," Brenner admitted. His confused expression made Lauren laugh.

"It's a blue phone booth that travels through time and space. Amy's neighbor has one, but it's not a pay phone."

"Okay..." Brenner stopped at a red light. "You can photograph a time-traveling spaceship, but not a pay phone?"

"About sums it up." Lauren stared at the phone in her lap. "I have to hand it to the Wizard. To get the next hashtag, I have to text her a picture of a pay phone...taken with a smartphone...which is exactly why pay phones are extinct." Her phone lit up with another text alert.

Amy: I have an idea. Confirming details.

Ivy: !!!

Lauren stretched her neck from side to side and fired

off a brief reply.

Lauren: Fingers crossed.

Amy: Stand by.

"Amy's checking on a lead." Lauren pointed to a strip mall up ahead and said, "How about we pull over and wait for her text."

"Sounds good," Brenner said as the traffic light turned green. He entered the parking lot and pulled into a well-lit space. In a series of fluid motions, he lowered their windows, turned off the engine, unbuckled his seat belt, and shifted in his seat to face Lauren. "You doing okay?" Brenner extended his arm over the center console and offered his hand.

"Yes." She put her phone in one of the cupholders between them, took off her seat belt, angled herself toward Brenner, and interlaced their fingers. Lauren didn't want to recheck the standings or spend this time complaining about the turn of events. Easy come, easy go. She'd gone further in the contest than she'd thought possible, and she was getting to know her own "hottie in the wild." She leaned over the console and gave Brenner a quick kiss on the lips. "Thanks for being such a good sport."

He returned her kiss. "Finding a pay phone is a tough one, but hanging out with you is no hardship. And the contest isn't over yet."

Lauren looked at the clock on the dashboard. "I have two hours to send in three pictures."

"You got this." He squeezed her fingers and said, "I'm sure Amy's lead is solid."

Lauren nodded. "There's still time." She refused to give up on the contest, and if the next two hours were anything like the last ten, it could happen. "After tonight, I know anything is possible."

"Are Scott and Ivy parked somewhere waiting for Amy's text or are they still out looking for a pay phone?"

"They're probably parked somewhere…making out," Lauren joked. "Not that I blame them. There are worse ways to kill time."

"They may be on to something." Brenner leaned toward her in the passenger seat, and as soon as their lips met, Lauren's phone signaled a new text.

Groaning at the timing, Lauren reached for her phone and said, "Hold that thought."

"No problem." Brenner let go of her hand and said, "It better be Amy, though."

She laughed and lifted her phone from the cupholder. "It is." Lauren read the text out loud:

Amy: From Susan:

The pool hall on Marlwood has one. Open 24/7.

Amy forwarded a map link and the texts from Susan:

It's in the hallway with bathrooms.

Phone works.

Tell Lauren I said good luck.

Keep me posted.

Lauren silently reread the texts, sighing in relief. "Depending on the condition of the pay phone near the pool hall bathrooms, I might kiss it." She opened the map link, pulling up directions to the pool hall.

Brenner started his truck and reached for his seat belt. "Our adventure continues." He turned his head and smiled at Lauren. "Rain check on the kiss?"

"Nope." Lauren leaned over the truck's console and made her intentions clear.

Brenner met her halfway, his low moan making her insides surge. Lauren put her hand on his wrist, and her fingers traveled up his arm and grabbed his shoulder. Brenner took her cue and gripped her waist. The kiss conveyed their mutual attraction, and in waves, it deepened, promised, and lingered. Her hand wandered to his neck and jaw, and she felt his heartbeat pounding against her fingertips. They slowly pulled away from each other but kept their faces close. Brenner's gaze shifted from her eyes to her mouth to the skin below her ear. His lips lowered to her earlobe and traveled south. Lauren's body tensed, and Brenner immediately gave her space.

"Do not kiss my neck right now." Lauren pushed herself back to the passenger seat. "I will never get out of your truck."

"Good to know." Brenner shifted back into his seat and clutched the steering wheel. "I'll be sure to remember that."

"Please do." Lauren settled in her seat and checked the clock on the dashboard. "This is crazy. About seven hours ago, I hid in a ladies' room to avoid you."

Brenner smiled. "Well, lucky for me you didn't have that kind of time."

"True." Lauren buckled up and said, "I'm curious why you didn't run the other way when you had the chance."

"I've never met anyone like you." Brenner pulled through the empty parking lot. "I knew then I wanted to know more about you."

"We met under unusual circumstances." When the turn-by-turn directions on the map app began, Lauren plugged her phone in Brenner's charger and laid it on his console so he could follow the navigation prompts. "It's not how I usually conduct myself in public." She had to laugh. Sneaking a picture of a hot guy was perfectly acceptable behavior compared to some of the tasks she'd done since leaving Barkley's.

"I'm sorry Jess embarrassed you." Lauren waited for the *but* in his sentence, but it never came. "I was flattered you found me attractive enough for your photo, and now I know what it takes to send the Wizard a picture." Brenner pulled onto the street and set out for the pool hall. "I was impressed. You saw an opportunity to move the needle on your goal and went for it. You let Sully and me join the fun, and you've kept your cool despite all the twists and turns. Tonight's been nothing but surprises. Dumpsters, hospitals, sexy tattoos…" When Lauren met his eyes, Brenner said, "By far, my favorite surprise is you in the seat beside me."

Lauren knew she'd replay that sentence in her head for quite some time. Brenner's sweet words were followed by a sexy smile, and she needed to pump the breaks on the swooning. She was aware of her propensity for falling too fast and crashing too hard. When Josh broke up with her, Lauren retreated to the corner of her couch with a box of tissues and two remote controls. She was only twenty minutes into her solo pity party when her apartment was ambushed. Ivy and Amy were armed with Prosecco, Halo Top ice cream, under-eye gel packs, and a tote bag filled with rapid-fire Nerf guns and foam darts. This wasn't the first time she'd been the recipient of a pop-up pity party, but she hadn't seen this one coming.

Ivy set the plastic guns next to Lauren on the couch and went to the kitchen to pour a round of drinks, the first of many. Amy crossed the living room and stood in front of the balcony's sliding glass doors. In one hand, she held the targets, rolled up and secured tightly with a rubber band. Amy forced the rubber band down the roll and laid the targets face down on the carpet.

Ivy appeared from the kitchen and placed a very generous pour of Prosecco, a pint of sea salt caramel, and a spoon on the coffee table in front of Lauren. "Breakfast of champions, lovey." She handed a drink to Amy, and they both turned to face Lauren on the couch.

Ivy raised her glass in the air. "May you never forget what is worth remembering or remember what is best forgotten."

"To getting over him." Amy lifted her drink. "It won't happen tonight or tomorrow, but your heart will eventually agree with your brain."

"Thank you. Both." Lauren was embarrassed by her brittle voice but continued. "I'm glad you came."

"Like we'd be anywhere else right now." Amy stuck the first target to the sliding glass door with blue painter's tape. Lauren wasn't surprised to see a digital illustration of a decayed zombie crawling out of a grave. Previous novelty targets included an angry squirrel holding a gun sideways and a massive kraken wrapping its tentacles around a pirate ship, its eyeball and suckers worth bonus points. Ivy preferred the shooting games: chip shots, pocket pool, sinking battleships. Usually, Lauren played along, not particular about the target, but always grateful for Amy's labor of love. "Gun Fun" was a hit at any party but was especially appreciated by friends in need of distraction, entertainment, and/or "magic bullet therapy." Amy believed shooting dart guns was a fun, practical way to relieve stress. Lauren had to agree.

Beside the zombie target, Amy hung up a target that broke from all tradition: an old Tom Brady ad for UGGs for men. Lauren nearly spit out her Prosecco.

"Don't choke on your Haterade," Amy said as she ripped more tape from the roll. "The GOAT didn't choose the UGG life. The UGG life chose him." After she secured the poster to the glass door, she made a production of showing her attraction to the famous quarterback. She rubbed her finger on the dimple in Tom Brady's chin. "Bitter envy follows greatness, baby. Don't take it personally." Amy blew the poster a kiss and finished taping the target to the glass door. Lauren set down her stemless champagne flute and looked through the plastic arsenal in the tote bag. She loaded three suction cup darts into a yellow and orange Nerf gun. It took considerable effort to untangle her legs from her quilt, but soon Lauren was standing up with her gun's laser beam focused on the quarterback's left foot. The red dot moved from the luxurious suede slipper to the sensible rubber sole, to the comfy, cozy wool lining engineered to feel like genuine shearling.

Amy pointed to the pile of targets on the floor. "Don't you want to see all your options before you take out my man's house shoes?"

"No thanks." Lauren squeezed the plastic trigger, and three foam darts shot across her living room and bounced off Tom Brady's left foot. "Such a wonderful, selfless thought. I know you love him."

"Yes, but I love you more." Amy picked up a bullseye target for Ivy from the pile on the floor. "If you want the one for Stetson Cologne, give a shout."

After an hour of shooting targets, drinking Prosecco, and requesting break-up anthems from Alexa, the friends settled into Lauren's sectional sofa. Ivy's irritation with the suction darts not sticking to the paper targets sparked a "first-world problem" conversation: no Wi-Fi, slow Wi-Fi, sunlight glare on screens, autocorrect, talk-to-text fails, wait…an app is missing, but which one? Ivy lamented about a software glitch in her first smartphone; she'd had to force a factory reset. Rebooting the original operating software fixed the problem, but all the data, apps, and settings on her phone were erased.

"And this was back before the cloud. It was gone. Forever," Ivy said. There was a collective cry of empathy for lost contacts, files, photos, and videos. In addition to Ivy's data, everything her phone had "learned" through user interface and software updates was deleted, meaning the phone operated like it did when it left the factory. "I had to go in and change every single setting. Again." Ivy opened a beauty treatment and stuck the gel-filled paisleys under her eyes. "Which is fun when it's a brand-new phone, but I spent forever tweaking things and had to start from scratch with no warning."

As Ivy grumbled about resetting how her phone looked, sounded, connected, searched, notified, sorted, saved, backed up, etc., Lauren opened and applied a set of the puffy gel pads under her eyes. She snuggled under her quilt and closed her eyes, delighting in the feel of the Prosecco's bubbles and the eye gel's tingling sensation. Amy and Ivy moved on to other first-world problems, but Lauren's thoughts stayed with default settings.

Perhaps getting dumped was the emotional equivalent of a factory reset. Lauren imagined her heart had an operating system like the one running her smartphone. After a year of "Girlfriend OS" updates, Lauren had become intuitive, efficient, and highly secure in her relationship with Josh. He'd been her go-to for good news, sick days, romantic evenings, future plans. And without warning, he was no longer accessible, and she was overwhelmed by the number of adjustments she had to make because he'd unexpectedly vanished.

Lauren snapped out of memory lane when her phone received several text messages in a row. She looked over at Brenner who was still following the GPS to the pool hall.

Brenner took his right hand off the steering wheel to hand her the phone. "Amy's name popped up with the texts."

Lauren opened the messages and read them to Brenner:

Amy: Cool if I meet you there?

Amy: I want to see you.

Amy: And Ivy.

Amy: And the menfolk you've collected tonight.

Ivy: !!! YAY !!!

Amy: Susan told me more about this pay phone.

Amy: I want to see it for myself.

CHAPTER SIXTEEN

Brenner

BRENNER WAS STUNNED TO SEE SO MANY VEHICLES IN A parking lot at half-past three on a Saturday morning. He pointed to the "Always Open" sign glowing in red cursive neon as he drove his truck past the entrance. Once he'd pulled into a parking space, Lauren unbuckled her seat belt.

"I've lived here a long time," she said, staring out her window. "I never knew this was a thing."

"Another surprise." Brenner turned off his truck's engine and said, "Let's go find the Wizard a pay phone."

They held hands as they walked across the parking lot and into Long Shots Billiards & Darts. Out of habit, Brenner memorized the exit locations and scanned the large space for suspicious activity. Two rows of pool tables divided the room, with four games underway. He took in the low-hung, green-glass pendant lights above each table, wooden cue racks, neon signs, and flat-screen televisions on the walls. Lauren squeezed his fingers before letting go of his hand. She pointed to the sign for the restrooms, and Brenner followed her past several vacant high-top tables until they reached the far side of the bar. The bathroom sign was hung above a set of saloon doors, and Lauren pushed one aside to enter a hallway. Brenner was right behind her, so when Lauren stopped dead in her tracks, he plowed into her back and nearly knocked her down.

"Sorry," they said to each other at the same time.

Lauren pointed a shaking finger ahead of her and said, "Brenner, look."

As if he could miss the iconic bright red British telephone booth nestled in an alcove at the end of the hallway. Stepping around Lauren, Brenner jogged the distance to knock his knuckles against the cast-iron sides. He pointed to the domed roof and said, "It has the crown and everything." Brenner turned back to look at Lauren who was still frozen in place.

"I was expecting a busted-up metal box…hanging crooked on a wall." She slowly pulled her phone out of her back pocket and continued walking down the hallway.

The unfiltered awe and relief on Lauren's face pulled Brenner's attention away from the phone booth. He'd only known her for eight hours or so, but in his mind, she'd never looked more beautiful. Brenner took a picture of Lauren with his phone, capturing the astonishment and wonder in her eyes. He put his phone away and opened the booth's door. "And the surprises keep coming."

Lauren laughed. "I can't believe it." As Brenner held the door open, she took multiple pictures with her phone, both close-ups and wide-angle shots. She exited the booth to stand close to Brenner, angling her phone so they could both see her screen. She swiped through the photos, pausing on an image when Brenner pointed to her phone.

"That's the one." He waved his finger across the image,

pointing out the details in the picture: a sleek black handset with a silver armored cord resting in its handle, coin slots, a keypad, and the coin return in the corner. Payment instructions were displayed in a silver frame, centered above a narrow shelf built into the side of the booth. "It's perfect," Brenner said.

"I agree." Lauren texted the picture to the Wizard and kissed Brenner on the cheek. As she turned away, his fingers lightly pressed on her jaw, redirecting her mouth to his. Their kiss was interrupted by a high-pitched shriek.

"Are you kidding me right now?" Ivy's words echoed off the hallway.

"What the—" Scott was clearly as surprised as the rest of them. He looked at Brenner and said, "Your woman is going to win this thing!"

"Damn straight." Brenner winked at Lauren, smiling when she blushed. He doubted seeing her cheeks flush would ever get old.

Ivy asked, "Has the Wizard seen this?" as she took her own pictures of the phone booth.

"I texted her right before you walked back here." Lauren showed Ivy and Scott the picture she sent the Wizard.

"Well done, you." Ivy hugged Lauren and said, "You'll be back on top after she gets a load of this bad boy." Ivy took a selfie in front of the red booth before tugging Scott close for a few more pictures. She handed him her phone, and said, "Your long arm is my new selfie stick, and I love it. Get as much of the booth as you can." Ivy blew a kiss to Scott and added, "Please."

"Anything for you, my lady," Scott said. He extended his arm and took several pictures before returning the phone to Ivy. Once she was content with the photos, Scott motioned for Brenner and Lauren to join them. "Let's get one of all of us."

Brenner noted the time on his watch and determined Lauren had a little over an hour to get the last two hashtags, and he was confident the next challenge was coming. As the four friends posed for a picture, Brenner recalled other times his photo had been taken since planning to meet Sully for a few rounds of beer: the covert #HitW entry, the group shot taken with a Polaroid at the bar, a few selfies with Lauren at the schoolhouse, and now their accidental double date.

The saloon doors swung open again, and a slender brunette in dark jeans and a turtleneck rushed down the hallway, squealing in excitement.

Lauren said, "Guys, this is Amy."

"Can you believe this pay phone?" Amy asked as she hugged Ivy and Lauren. "You already sent a picture?"

"Just now, yes. Thanks for joining the fun."

"Like I'd miss watching you win ten large." Amy pointed to Lauren's phone. "Do you have the next hashtag?"

Lauren knew she didn't but checked the screen anyway. "No, but it should be on its way. I only sent the picture a minute ago. Can't imagine why it wouldn't be approved."

"I agree." Amy turned to face Brenner and Scott. "And here we have the hottie and the hero, correct?"

Lauren made the introductions. Brenner didn't usually bust out his dimple on demand, but he hoped Amy would find it endearing. He extended his palm for a handshake, and said, "Hello, Amy. I've been looking forward to meeting you."

"Polite, too?" Amy made a production of sizing him

up before shaking his hand. "I'm watching you, Hashtag Hottie." Amy took a few steps and stood in front of Scott. "You must be the one wearing dog tags."

"Correct." He shook her hand and said, "Scott Sullivan, but friends call me Sully."

"Okay, Sully. Here's the thing: I wasn't in the group picture, so you'll have to retake it."

"Yes, ma'am." Scott raised his phone to take another picture as Amy positioned herself in the middle of the group.

"Look how high he gets the camera!" said Amy. "Now tilt it down a bit…a little more…perfect. Hold it there for one more second." Amy finger-combed her bangs and smoothed the ends of her hair. When she was happy with her appearance on the screen, she said, "Okay, go."

Scott took three pictures and handed Amy his phone to look at them.

"Perfect." Amy zoomed in on each face. "Cool if I send them to my phone?"

"Of course," Scott said.

After Amy texted herself, she told the group, "While we're waiting…" She rummaged through her navy Coach bucket bag and lifted out a matching wallet. She took a folded piece of paper and a quarter from the zippered pouch. "I was told this booth has a special feature. Do you mind if I try to find it while we wait for the next text?"

"Is it some kind of underground Uber?" Ivy asked. "Driving us to a fight club? Or a VIP lounge? Or what's that white-attire dinner party?"

"Dîner en Blanc," said Lauren. "I wish, but that probably isn't happening at three forty-five in the morning."

"Wait…what?" asked Scott. He looked at Brenner, who

was equally confused.

Brenner looked at Lauren and said, "Please tell me 'underground Uber' isn't a thing."

"I've never heard of it," Lauren shrugged her shoulders. "But it wouldn't surprise me. A lot of apps are used for keeping secrets." She pointed to the paper and quarter Amy was holding. "This is much lower tech, but it works."

Amy returned her wallet to the depths of her purse, opened the phone booth's door, and approached the pay phone while dramatically unfolding the paper. "Honestly, I don't know what happens, but let's find out." She set the paper down on the narrow shelf and lifted the handset off the cradle. Instead of placing the receiver against her ear, she held it out so they all could hear the steady, monotonous dial tone. The sound ended once Amy pushed her quarter into the coin slot. She read from the creased paper, saying the numbers out loud as she pressed the buttons on the keypad. "Nine, three, four, one, one, one, two, zero, zero, seven." The call connected, and the quarter slid to the collection box, landing with a muted chink.

After ringing twice, a high-pitched, singsongy feminine voice answered the line. "Rhythm is our business…"

"…and business sure is swell," Amy read.

"How many?"

"Five, please."

"Sit tight, sister." The operator ended the call with a click, and Amy waited until she heard the dial tone before hanging up. As soon as the handset was returned to its cradle, the sound of deadbolts sliding open echoed through the steel and glass structure. The panel on the far side shifted to the right, revealing a gap in the wall.

"Oh, hell no." Amy bolted out of the phone booth and

hid behind Lauren.

As soon as Brenner had heard the metal scraping of keys and locks, he'd been on alert. He noticed Scott scanning the phone booth with wide eyes, which Brenner found somewhat comforting. He and Scott were analyzing possible threats when the reason for the noise and movement became evident. The far side of the phone booth was swinging on hidden hinges into the room behind it.

"Look, Amy!" Ivy pointed to the phone booth. "It's a hidden door! How cool is that?"

"Not as cool as some heads-up would've been, but yeah." Amy peered over Lauren's shoulder. "Hidden doors are cool."

"It probably leads to a bar," Scott said. He looked at Brenner and jerked his head toward the opening. "But we better make sure this passage is used for good, not evil."

"Whatever, Sully. You just want to nerd out over hidden hardware." Brenner followed Scott into the phone booth and laughed when his friend stopped to take a picture of the flush doorjamb. They'd seen their share of secret tunnels on deployment, used for smuggling everything from cigarettes to women. Out of habit, he hunched down to avoid a low ceiling once the opening was wide enough to pass. He assumed he'd find another narrow, dirty, poorly lit corridor. When Brenner crossed the threshold, he triggered a pair of motion-activated light fixtures. He rose to his full height and scanned his surroundings.

Brenner knew the phone booth wasn't a magical portal, but it was as if he'd been dropped into the alleyway behind an inner-city apartment building. His best guess was he was standing at the top of what had once been a stairwell. All four walls were weathered-brick facades, complete with cracked mortar, concrete sills, and peeling paint. The windows were covered in props: air-conditioner units, flower boxes, broken blinds, black-out curtains, party lights, and championship pennants. It took longer than he'd admit to realize he was standing on the grated metal landing of a residential fire escape. Brenner quickly confirmed it was bolted to the brick facade behind him. The balcony landing, wrought iron railing, and secured drop ladder were every bit as authentic as the red British phone booth on the other side of the wall.

Brenner found his voice. "Sully, you have to come see this, brother."

"They used pivot hinges," Scott said as he needlessly ducked down while walking through the door. He was looking at his phone, scrolling through the pictures he'd taken. "My kneecaps have the same design—" Scott looked up and was stunned into silence for several moments. He put his hand on Brenner's shoulder and said, "There's a chance I'm hallucinating, B."

"I see it too, Sully."

Brenner watched Scott shake off the bewilderment and analyze the facts. "I'll check out the lower level." He walked three steps to the right side of the balcony and unhooked the drop ladder from the railing. He let it slide down, and the metal on metal screech had both men cringing. "They even got that right." Scott climbed down the ladder and did a sweep of the lower level. "Makes me miss New York. All they're missing is the traffic noise, light pollution, mountains of trash, and the smell of fresh bagels in the morning." After his second lap around the "alley," he reported, "All clear."

"Copy that." Brenner didn't want to ruin the surprise,

so when he ducked his head through the opening, he simply said, "The landing on this side is narrow, so you'll have to make your way to Scott one at a time."

Ivy was the first through the secret door. Startled, she grabbed the balcony's railing with both hands and asked, "Did we crash a movie set?"

"More like dinner theater," Scott said from below. "Reminds me of when I agreed to be Romeo's understudy to impress a girl." He lowered himself onto one knee and stacked his hands over his heart. To Ivy, he declared, "'Did my heart love till now? Forswear it, sight! For I ne'er saw true beauty till this night.'"

"You sweet, sexy man." Ivy leaned over the balcony and blew Scott a kiss. "I memorized some Shakespeare too: 'And though she be but little, she is fierce.'"

CHAPTER SEVENTEEN

Lauren

AMY SHOOK HER HEAD. SCOTT AND IVY'S BANTER HAD carried through the hidden opening in the phone booth. "Have they been like this all night?"

"Reciting Shakespeare is new, but yes." Lauren nodded and said, "They've been flirting since they met at Barkley's."

Brenner was leaning against the secret door and looking into the space hidden behind the wall. Amy waved a finger between him and Lauren. "And how long have you two been flirting?"

"It's all a blur." Lauren thought back on the evening and smiled at Brenner. "I'd say somewhere between the anchor and the helicopter...we talked about our tattoos and kissed at the gas station."

Amy pretended she'd gotten faint and dramatically fell into the side of the phone booth. "My lands! I'm swooning!"

"Shut up." Lauren laughed at her friend's antics. "It was sweet."

"Glad to hear it," said Brenner. Amy stood up straight and put a hand on Lauren's shoulder. "Now normally, I'd discourage you from making out against a gas pump, but in this case, I am seriously happy for you."

Lauren shook her head. "It was amazing, but we were hardly making out against the gas pump."

"I was trying to be a gentleman." Brenner ducked his head in through the doorway. "You sound disappointed."

"You heard the part where I said it was amazing?"

"You bet I did."

"Ugh. You kids are giving me cavities." Amy tried to look behind Brenner, but his body blocked the passage. "So, what's going on back there?"

"It's not what you'd expect, but that seems to be the theme of this adventure." Brenner leaned back through the opening and looked to the left. He moved to the side, making room for Amy. "Ivy's on her way down. Would you like to go next?"

Instead of answering Brenner, Amy looked back at Lauren, "Still no word from the Wizard?"

Lauren looked down at her phone. "Still no word."

"Thanks for being cool about the detour. It's all hands on deck once you get the next hashtag."

"I know, and this is way more fun than staring at my phone in the parking lot." While Amy passed through the opening, Lauren crossed the booth's interior to stand by Brenner. They shared an affectionate smile, but the moment was ruined by Amy's loud gasp. Lauren shook her head and asked, "You're not even going to give me a hint?"

"Nope." Brenner stepped back into the phone booth. "You should be surprised like the rest of us, but I will say it's every bit as random as the hashtags we've been chasing." He reached for her hand and interlaced their fingers. "You doing okay?"

Lauren took a deep breath, considering her answer before she spoke. "I'd be better if the Wizard would send number eleven." With a little more than an hour left until the deadline, she needed the next hashtag immediately. She nodded toward the pay phone beside her and said, "I thought this would be another fast yes, but I've got nothing." The Hashtag Hunt had taught Lauren anything was possible, but she was feeling the pressure of racing the clock. "I should apologize now for anything I may say or do if I don't get a text in the next five minutes."

"You'll get one." Brenner rubbed one of her cheeks with his thumb. "She's probably texting other contestants, verifying a ton of helicopter entries."

"Thank you for saying that." Lauren tugged him in for a quick hug, but learned—and loved that—there was nothing quick about hugging Brenner. It was as if neither of them wanted to let go. After all the frantic hashtag hunting, she welcomed this quiet, peaceful moment inside the British phone booth. As much as she needed to get started on the next challenge, she also wanted to soak in this time with her favorite hottie.

Brenner kissed her forehead. "When Sully asked me to grab a beer, I had no idea where the night would lead."

"I know what you mean." Lauren couldn't contain her smile. "I entered this contest on a whim, and the next thing I know, I'm standing in a phone booth with a secret passage. I've trespassed a few times, witnessed a heart transport, unzipped my jeans to photograph my tattoo, and spent the majority of the Hashtag Hunt with a hottie." She hugged Brenner tight and looked him in the eyes. "Meeting you is the only thing that's happened that makes sense."

"I wish I could kiss you right now," Brenner murmured.

"You can." Lauren's heart raced. "You can kiss me anytime you want, for the record."

"I am a lucky man." Brenner gently moved Lauren toward the only side of the booth not used as a door, pay phone station, or a hidden tunnel. He grabbed her by the waist and pressed her against the glass and metal panel. "You are so beautiful."

After all the running around she'd done since the contest started, Lauren didn't feel beautiful, but years ago, Ivy had taught her how to take a compliment. "Just say, 'Thank you,' and smile. I meant what I said, even if you don't agree." Ivy explained at the time, "You're basically calling me a liar right after I say something nice to you. Cut that shit out." Lauren smiled at the memory.

Brenner continued, "Smart, kind, funny, driven, and so very beautiful."

All Lauren could manage was a breathy, "Thank you."

"You're welcome." Brenner smiled at her response, and Lauren was glad she hadn't brushed off his compliments. He cupped her chin with one hand and tilted her face up toward his. "So, I can kiss you anytime I want?"

Lauren nodded because she no longer trusted herself to speak. He looked at her as if she were the only person in the world, and with the grip on her chin, he controlled the kiss from start to finish. As their kiss slowed down, Lauren's heart rate sped up, and she was sure Brenner could hear her heart pounding. She wrapped her arms around his neck, keeping him close, but their bodies jerked away from each other when a high-pitched whistle blasted from the other side of the wall.

"That'd be Sully's famous wolf whistle," Brenner said. "It must be your turn." He tucked a few wayward strands of her hair behind an ear. "Ready to see what's behind door number two?" He stepped back so Lauren could approach the secret opening.

Lauren marveled at Brenner's willingness to support her in this bizarre contest. Before she crossed the threshold, Lauren turned toward him and said, "Thank you again for all the help, compliments, encouragement, the driving, the kissing...all of it. If I am out of the contest, I'll need your breathing techniques too."

"If it comes to that, I'm here for you." Brenner squeezed her palm. "But no way are you out of the contest. You'll see."

Lauren grabbed the front of his shirt and tugged him down for a kiss. "Your optimism gives me strength," she said. "When this is all over, I'll spoil you with Shady Brady memes and Slim Jims."

"Can't wait." Brenner released Lauren's hand as she walked through the hidden passage.

Lauren didn't know where to look first: the brick walls, the randomly decorated windows, the fire escape beneath her feet, or the steep ladder between her and her friends.

"Crazy, right?" Brenner had followed her onto the landing and leaned against the railing.

Amy shouted up from below, "It's not every day you get to stroll through an eighties pool hall, a British phone booth, and now," she gestured to the walls surrounding them, "the Lower East Side in under ten minutes."

Lauren looked down from the balcony and said, "I haven't been in so many places at once since Epcot."

Brenner laughed. "I wonder what's next."

Lauren was having a difficult time getting her mind around the view. She'd been to a few unusual places since the Hashtag Hunt began, but walking through a phone booth onto a fire escape was more astonishing than the old schoolhouse or hospital rooftop. "Of all the things I've seen tonight, why is this the most unexpected?" she asked the group.

"Nothing beats Scott jumping over that deer," Ivy said, "so the award for biggest surprise goes to him."

"Wait," said Amy. "What?"

"I did not jump over a deer," Scott said to Amy. "I jumped away from one."

"You basically flew into Brenner's truck," Ivy teased. "Like you were wearing rocket boots."

"Rocket boots can't store enough fuel to work for more than a few seconds," said Scott. "They're cool, but not practical. I have hydraulic cylinders."

"Wait," Amy repeated. "What? I know I'm late to the party, but if we're deciding what's been the biggest shock, this conversation gets my vote." Amy pointed to the ladder and said to Lauren, "Hustle up, Laurenburger. Clock's ticking."

"Don't I know it," Lauren said as she carefully walked across the landing. When she grabbed the ladder's side rails, it occurred to Lauren that she'd never had to use a fire escape before, much less one attached to brick veneer by a handful of bolts. "This is safe, right?"

"Most fire escapes like this are rusted or falling away because they've been exposed to the elements for a hundred years. We're indoors, so it's in great condition," Brenner said. Once Lauren began climbing down, he made his way to the ladder. "And since it held Sully, it'll hold the rest of us."

"I can hear you, you know," Scott shouted up to

Brenner. "And thanks to the carbon fiber, I weigh much less than you ever will."

"So, to recap," Amy said, "you're not wearing rocket boots, but you do have hydraulics and carbon fiber."

Lauren listened to the conversation as she descended the ladder, and the confusion in Amy's voice made her laugh. "Clear as mud?" she asked over her shoulder.

"Help a girl out, Lauren." Amy asked, "What am I missing?"

"It's more about what I'm missing," Scott answered. "I wear prosthetics."

As Lauren stepped off the ladder, she turned and saw Scott raising the hems on his jeans and revealing his silver legs.

Lauren couldn't miss the side-eye Amy gave Ivy. "Oh, I'm sorry! I had no idea—" Amy began.

"Please don't be sorry," Scott interrupted. "These legs are quite the upgrade. They have cutting-edge technology and military-grade bionics."

"But no rocket boosters?" Amy confirmed. "Bummer."

"Agreed," Scott said. "But things can get a little sci-fi from time to time."

"Like jumping away from a deer into a truck," Amy clarified. "This is a story I want to hear, but it'll have to wait until after the contest."

Brenner made quick work of climbing down the ladder and joined the others in the middle of the alleyway. He looked around the lower level and asked, "So what do we do now?"

"I don't know," Scott said. "I'm stumped." He laughed at his own joke. "Get it? Stumped?"

Lauren's giggle bubbled out. "Sorry, I shouldn't laugh,

but that was funny."

"As long as the amputee is the one cracking the jokes, you can laugh all you want," Scott said with a wink.

"Dad jokes and amputee jokes?" Ivy groaned. "It's amazing that you've kept your sense of humor, but you could use better material."

"I'll get right on that. You can count on me." Scott lifted his hands and splayed his fingers wide. "But only up to ten."

Amy and Lauren laughed at his joke, and Ivy shook her head. "Don't encourage him."

Brenner asked Lauren, "Do you get a good signal down here?"

She pulled her phone out of her back pocket and looked at the screen. Instead of looking at the tiny bars in the upper left corner, she stared at the time displayed in the center. "I only have an hour left."

"But do you have a signal?" Ivy asked. "If not, we should go back to the pool hall."

Lauren told the others there were two full bars, and she opened the #HashtagHunt app to confirm she could refresh the leaderboard. "I'm still in second place now."

"Let's find our way out of this alley," Brenner suggested. "Sully, any idea where we should look?"

While the others studied the walls surrounding them, Lauren continued to stare at her phone. She was running out of time. Her eyes got wet, and she blinked back the tears before her friends could see them fall. Lauren turned her back to the group, pretending to look for another secret door.

They searched the space for a few minutes before Amy pulled out her cell phone. "I may be waking her up, but I'm texting Susan. I know she didn't send us off to a dead end." Amy's thumbs flew over her screen. "We must be missing something."

As far as Lauren could tell, each wall on this level was solid, and she turned her attention to the cracked asphalt below her feet, the silver metal trash cans in the corner, and the empty bike rack centered under the fire escape's balcony. Scott pointed up to the hidden door they'd discovered. It was still open to the phone booth behind it.

"Do we need to make another phone call?" asked Ivy.

"No," Amy said. "Susan would've said to bring more than one quarter."

Scott walked to the drop ladder and said to Brenner, "Maybe it's like the Saudi general's panic room."

"Good thinking," Brenner said as Scott slid the drop ladder up the rails, raising it to its original position with another loud screech. As soon as it was secure, the phone booth's hidden door quickly swung the other way, closing the gap with a metallic clang that echoed throughout the alley.

"This is how idiots die in horror films." Lauren continued to look around the space, hoping something on the lower level had also shifted. "What if that was our only way out?"

Brenner put an arm around her shoulder and said, "Somebody spent a ridiculous amount of time and money designing and building all this, so it must lead to another location." Lauren quietly nodded, and he added, "The way *in* and the way *through* are real, and so is the way *out*. We'll find it."

CHAPTER EIGHTEEN

Brenner

WHEN LAUREN'S PAY PHONE PICTURE WASN'T INSTANTLY approved, Brenner assumed she'd receive another "photo authentication required" message from the Wizard. It wasn't as remarkable as the AirMedic helicopter taking flight, but he could see if she needed to prove she hadn't sent in a stock photo of a British phone booth. With fewer contestants remaining in the Hashtag Hunt, the response rate should have been faster...and even if Lauren had been unjustly disqualified, she deserved to know immediately.

Brenner watched Lauren shift her gaze from the brick walls to the fire escape before she met his eyes. He gave her a wink and a smile, hoping his unease about the situation wasn't obvious. He wanted to encourage Lauren, but they were trapped in an indoor alley with an hour left in the contest. Brenner took a few moments for an intentional meditation, another technique his counselor suggested to "achieve a mentally clear and emotionally calm state." The trick was focusing the mind on something very specific. And at the moment, his mind was explicitly focused on kicking the Wizard's scrawny ass.

Brenner had never believed the person behind the Hashtag Hunt was the beautiful steampunk woman in the profile picture. In his mind, the Wizard was a thirty-something basement-dweller surrounded by monitors and Mountain Dew. Brenner closed his eyes, took a deep breath, and visualized yanking the Wizard out of an expensive gaming chair by his dirty neckbeard. He'd threaten to pour half-empty soda bottles over every motherboard in the house until Lauren received an apology, an explanation, the eleventh hashtag, and time back on the clock. The mental play-by-play was surprisingly relaxing, but his silent meditation was disrupted by a loud shout from Sully.

Scott was pointing to a large section of bricks in front of him. "Alright! Here we go!" he exclaimed as a row of veneer slid smoothly to the right, revealing a narrow slit behind the wall.

"A speakeasy grill! Are you kidding me?" Amy squealed and fished her phone out of her purse. She snapped a few pictures of the peephole but immediately stopped when the metal hatch was forcefully shoved to the side. Jazz music wafted through the small opening, and a pair of hooded eyes began studying each of them in turn. Brenner noticed how the piercing stare softened when it landed on Amy.

A husky voice addressed everyone, but the eyes never left Amy. "You must be the party of five."

"That's us." Amy took a step closer to the peephole and maintained eye contact with the bouncer. They stared at each other for several seconds before she said, "If you're waiting on a secret handshake or something, I got nothing."

"Secret handshake?" Laugh lines appeared at the corners of his eyes.

"Or secret password or secret knock, or whatever. I was only informed about the phone call." Amy gestured to her friends and said, "And not to be rude, but we're kind of in a hurry here."

"What's the rush?" Eyebrows furrowed as the gaze cut to Brenner and moved to Scott.

Amy pointed at Lauren. "She's in a contest and as soon as she gets a hashtag, we'll have to book it out of here, probably. Hopefully number eleven is '#Speakeasy.'"

"I'm sorry to hear you can't stay long, kitten, but you lost me at hashtag." A well-hidden pocket door quickly slid into the brick wall, and the speakeasy's jazz music poured into the alleyway. A barrel-chested man in a tailored suit walked through the doorway and winked at Amy. "Welcome to the Back Alley Barrelhouse. Please come back when you have more time."

"You can count on it." Amy took a few steps toward the door and stopped when she was beside the bouncer. "What's your name, big guy?"

"They call me Moose," he said with a shrug. "Always have."

"It suits you. I like it." Brenner watched Amy dig through her purse and pull something from its depths. "In case we don't get to chat, here's how to get ahold of me later."

Moose's gaze swept over her. "I would love to get ahold of you later…" he looked down to read the business card as she handed it to him, "Amy." Brenner checked Lauren's and Ivy's reactions to Moose's bold flirting, but their knowing smirks suggested the man had met his match.

"Yeah, you look like trouble," Amy said. "Call me."

With a wink and a wave goodbye, she passed through the doorway.

"This is so exciting!" Ivy clapped her hands and grinned at Lauren. "Can you believe it?" Brenner wasn't sure if she was talking about the secret bar or about what had just gone down between Amy and Moose. "Come on!" she said. She smiled at the bouncer as she passed into the speakeasy.

Brenner suggested Lauren go in next. "You should catch up with your friends. Sully will want to get a good look at this pocket door."

"He's not wrong," Scott said. "I've never seen one installed in brick, but I'll be quick, promise."

"Take your time. There's no rush," Lauren said, waving her phone. "See you inside."

After she left the alley, Moose pulled the pocket door out several inches, and Scott studied the mechanics.

"Looks like galvanized panels in a cavity wall," he said. "Which explains the soundproofing."

Moose pointed to where the door hung from the top jamb. "It's a two-piece track system with precision ground ball bearings." They spent a few minutes admiring the door's engineering and execution. It reminded Brenner of when his dad would check under the hoods of '67 Cobras and '71 Stingrays and geek out at car shows.

"If you like hidden passages, you'll get a kick out of the trap doors and secret compartments in this building," Moose said. "Come back when you can, and I'll show you around."

"Seriously? Of course I want in on that. Thanks, man." Scott initiated the modern-day bro hug of clasped hands, leaning torsos, and back slapping. "I can't wait."

"Anytime." Moose followed Scott and Brenner through

the opening in the wall and slid the door closed behind them. "I hope you enjoy your time here, however long it lasts." They thanked him and entered the darkened speakeasy, both men sweeping the area out of habit.

The shiplap walls were stained the same dark brown as the hardwood floors, and several strands of Edison string lights crisscrossed the ceiling. A jazz trio was in the far corner, and two couples were jitterbugging to their rendition of "Ain't Misbehavin'." Amy, Ivy, and Lauren were speaking with a woman dressed like a cigarette girl. As they joined the women, Brenner saw the cigars, matchbooks, chewing gum, candy bars, and playing cards displayed on the vintage black tray she carried by a neck strap. Her red, satin saloon-style minidress matched her pillbox hat perfectly, and she wore black fishnets.

"These must be the gents you mentioned." She waved at Brenner and Scott and said, "Party of five, follow me!" She escorted them to a large lounge opposite the dance floor with plush furniture grouped into various conversation areas. "Is this okay?" the cigarette girl asked, showing them a long, high-backed banquette, a pair of wingback chairs, and a steamer trunk serving as a coffee table. Everyone agreed it was more than okay, and the women shared the tufted velvet bench while each man sank into a soft leather chair. "Welcome to the Back Alley. I'm Hazel," she said. "You guys are first-timers, right?"

"Aw, how could you tell?" asked Scott.

"We probably look like the people at those break-out places." Amy finger-combed her bangs. "You know, where you pay money to be locked in a room and have an hour to escape."

"Speaking of having an hour," Ivy got Hazel's attention

and said, "we're in a scavenger hunt and expect the next clue any second." She squeezed Lauren's knee twice and asked, "How do we get out of here?"

Hazel pointed to the far wall and said, "There's a back door and a small flight of steps up to the parking lot."

"That sounds way too simple," Scott said. "No offense."

"None taken. A few guests consider it quite the letdown after the phone booth and fire escape," Hazel smiled, "but most people are relieved it's so easy when it's time to go."

Amy looked around their seating area. "Is there a drink menu?"

"No," said Hazel. "We only serve gin and whiskey."

"You *only* serve gin and whiskey…" Amy checked the time on her phone, "at *four in the morning*?"

"Is that legal?" Ivy asked.

Hazel thumbed over her shoulder toward the bar and said, "No alcohol sales from five to six in the morning, but that's it. The bar's open the other twenty-three hours a day."

Brenner turned in his chair to study the set-up behind him. The Back Alley's bar consisted of a weather-beaten door laid across two whiskey barrels and an antique oak icebox against the wall. Instead of liquor bottles shelved behind the bar, dozens of mugs and teacups hung from little white hooks.

"We only serve shots of gin and whiskey." Hazel's explanation was obviously memorized from repetition, her voice falling flat as she said, "And they come in coffee cups for the gents and teacups for the dolls. There are no flappers, bartenders, or cocktails because the owner wants it to represent the secret bars that served the era's working class."

"That's really cool," said Ivy.

"Does a shot of whiskey cost thirty-five cents?" Amy joked. "Because that would make it extra authentic."

"The boss folded in a few modern-day touches," Moose said as he approached the group, "like air conditioning, Wi-Fi, and inflation." He leaned against Amy's side of the tall banquette and looked down at her. "You know your stuff."

"It's my favorite decade," Amy said with a shrug.

"And why's that?" Moose asked.

"Lots of reasons." Counting on her fingers, Amy listed off, "Women can vote, radio stations become a thing, Charles Lindbergh, Babe Ruth, the Harlem Renaissance." She switched hands and continued counting. "The NFL, the Tomb of the Unknown Soldier, *The Great Gatsby*, Albert Einstein wins the Nobel Prize, and Art Deco architecture…in no particular order. Except for the Nineteenth Amendment coming in at number one."

"But it wasn't all sunshine and rainbows, was it?" asked Moose. He followed her lead and counted on his fingers. "The Great Migration, five million KKK members, the Red Scare, the Wall Street bombing, immigration restrictions." Before he started counting on his other fingers, Moose stretched out his arms, gesturing at the speakeasy. "Prohibition, Al Capone, wide-spread corruption in law enforcement and politics, the stock market crash, and the Great Depression. The decade may have started with a roar, but it crashed and burned when it ended."

"Plenty of good and bad when it comes to progress," Amy agreed. "That's true for every decade since the Industrial Revolution. But the roaring twenties had the best style when it came to creativity and innovation."

Brenner and Lauren shared a smile, both clearly enjoying the banter between Moose and Amy.

"So who's behind all this?" Scott asked Moose. "The phone booth, the fire escape, the peephole, the pocket door… It's either installation art or someone's expensive labor of love."

"Aren't those the same thing?" Moose said with a chuckle. "There are a few urban legends about who did all this and why, but nobody knows for sure."

"So," Hazel said before clearing her throat. "Will it be gin or whiskey?"

"Right. Sorry." Lauren went first. "Whiskey, please."

"Neat or on the rocks?"

Lauren ordered her whiskey neat, and a round of "same" rose from the others. Brenner wasn't one to drink before oh-five-hundred, but he'd been going with the flow for nearly eight hours now. Hazel excused herself, promising to return shortly, and the musicians across the room began playing the jazz standard "Blue Skies."

"Care to dance, kitten?" Moose extended a massive palm toward Amy.

"Hold that thought, big guy." Leaning forward to see around Ivy, she looked at Lauren and asked, "Any word?" When Lauren shook her head, Amy rose from the banquette and took Moose's hand. "I'll fill you in on the Hashtag Hunt," she told him as they walked to the dance floor.

Ivy asked Scott if his legs were programmed to slow dance, and the next thing Brenner knew, he was alone with Lauren in their seating area. He left his leather wingback and joined her on the velvet banquette.

"How's your signal?" Brenner asked. "We are

underneath the parking lot."

Lauren checked the screen. "Two bars." Clutching the phone in her hand, she said, "Zero texts."

"It's coming," he said, despite feeling nervous himself. Brenner took a deep breath and visualized threatening to cut every power cord and connector cable in half while the Wizard begged for mercy. Brenner marveled at how quickly his anxiety eased once he began visualizing their confrontation about Lauren's pay phone picture. "The ringer's set to extra loud?"

Lauren confirmed the volume was up high and nodded. "Wait. Did you just say we're under the parking lot?" She looked at Brenner as she laid her phone on the steamer trunk.

"Pretty sure." Brenner nodded.

Lauren leaned against his shoulder and said, "I've never been in a speakeasy before."

"Me either," Brenner said, gently taking her hand. He interlaced their fingers and squeezed her palm. "Hopefully the next hashtag will be something we can find in here."

"I like our chances," Lauren replied, looking around the bar. "This place has lots of random."

Hazel returned, saying, "Here we go!" She'd left her big, black tray of cigars and candy at the bar in order to carry five cups on an oversized cutting board. She placed it carefully on the trunk and said, "A round of whiskeys, neat." Brenner smiled at the three dainty teacups on matching saucers and two thick, chipped, white coffee mugs. "Even the surprises have surprises," he said, handing Lauren a delicate cup and saucer, both white and covered in yellow daisies.

Before she took a sip of whiskey, Lauren held the

teacup in one hand and flipped the matching saucer over with the other. She showed Brenner the green shield and crown stamped on the bottom of the china. "I like learning about the maker's mark," she said as she returned the saucer to the trunk. After taking a sip of whiskey, Lauren set the teacup down and picked up her phone. She snuggled into Brenner's side, and he put his arm around her shoulder, nuzzled her hair with his chin, and watched her Google "Arzberg Bavaria porcelain." She tapped her thumb on a Wikipedia link, and as it was loading, a text from the Wizard appeared on the screen. They both sat up straight and bent over her phone to read the next challenge.

Challenge 11 of 12: #YOLO
Time Remaining: 0 hours and 48 minutes

Lauren looked over at the dance floor, and Brenner followed her gaze. Her friends were smiling at their dance partners, slowly swaying to the music. He thought she intended to take a picture of the couples slow dancing, but instead of alerting them about the hashtag, she opened her camera app and turned it to selfie mode.

Brenner was pretty sure he knew what YOLO meant, but as she shifted to face him, he asked anyway. "You only live once, right?"

Lauren used her left hand to get a handful of his Henley. "Right." She tugged him down by his shirt and passionately pressed her lips against his. With her right hand, she lifted the phone and took several photos of them kissing. Brenner was taken off guard by her spontaneous PDA, but he wasn't complaining—especially in light of the YOLO context. She slowly pulled away from their kiss and tucked herself back into his side.

"Wow." His heart was pounding, and he had to clear his throat before saying, "Thank you for that." He leaned forward to pick up his coffee mug. Lauren was scrolling through the pictures she'd just taken. "Are those for your private collection?" he teased before he swallowed his shot of whiskey.

Lauren giggled. "You bet. But first," she said, showing him the screen, "this one is my YOLO entry."

It was one of the first pictures she took, and it captured the look of surprise in Brenner's eyes and the look of affection in Lauren's. A red flag went up in Brenner's mind as the whiskey burned his throat. He returned his empty mug to the table, and said, "Wait," but he was too late. She'd already sent the picture of them kissing to the Wizard.

"What?" Lauren asked as she set her phone down and picked up her teacup. "I don't know what took so long, but I'm glad the hashtag was an easy one."

She looked so happy that Brenner didn't want to say what he was thinking, but he did anyway. "Won't a picture of me be a repeat entry since I was already in a hashtag picture?" He hated how the joy drained from her eyes.

The teacup slipped from her hand, and it shattered on the hardwood floor, covering her shoes in china shards and whiskey. "Oh my God," she gasped. "What have I done?"

CHAPTER NINETEEN

The Wizard

THERE WAS NO DOUBT IT WAS THE HOTTIE, BUT ALICE OPENED @laurenburger's #HitW entry and compared the photos anyway. She lowered her forehead to the boardroom table and cussed a blue streak.

"Language, A-Train! It can't possibly be that bad."

"Oh no?" Alice lifted her head and slid her iPad across the table toward her twin brother, Marc. He'd been lazily scrolling through his phone, and his eyes drifted from his screen to the tablet as it stopped in front of him. He gasped and sprung up so fast his chair slammed into the wall behind him. "You're right. I overreacted," Alice said. "It's no big, right?"

"How could this happen?" Marc plopped back into his chair and stared at the picture of Lauren Daniels kissing the hottie from hashtag number five. "She's been killing this contest. I had her going all the way." He pushed the iPad back to his sister with a loud groan. "I feel sick."

"Me too." Stiff from hours of hunching over the pile of electronics dubbed Mission Control, Alice stood up to stretch. "The Hashtag Hunt was an eight, maybe an eight-point-five. Once I disqualify Lauren, it'll drop to a negative fifty-six."

Marc nodded. "I would have rated the contest a solid nine until things went sideways with the helicopter pictures."

"Thank you…I think." Authenticating so many pictures of helicopters had taken extra time, but Alice had no regrets. Over a third of the contestants were disqualified, and dozens more withdrew voluntarily. The pay phone entries yielded similar results, and weeding out so many participants as the deadline approached made for a short list of contenders.

There were two rapid knocks before a stern voice carried through the office door. "Ms. Matthews?"

Ugh, this guy again, she thought. *Would it kill him to call me Alice?* Since the inauguration, she had repeatedly asked both members of her security team to drop the formalities, but the federal agents refused her request. Alice understood the First Family deserved respect, but at age nineteen, she was too old for *Miss*, and *Ms. Matthews* was her mother's name. Or at least it was before everyone in America started calling her Madam President.

"Come in," Alice said as she returned to her chair. The door opened, and one-half of her security team entered the boardroom. "Hello, Special Agent Marshall." *Two can play at this game.*

"Hello." Oliver Marshall greeted her with a stiff smile and then nodded toward her brother seated at the other end of the conference table. "Mr. Matthews. Good morning."

"Well, it was a great morning until my girl got herself disqualified," Marc said with a heavy sigh.

"Ah, and which girl is that?" Oliver turned his attention

to the flat-screen television hanging on the wall. The leaderboard was on display, and he said, "Gang's all here. Who do you mean?"

"I haven't updated the standings yet," Marc said. "I can't bring myself to do it."

"Why?" Oliver looked from Marc to Alice and back again. "What's happened?"

"This happened," Alice said. With a few clicks of her keyboard, the leaderboard was replaced with Lauren's #YOLO photograph on the flat screen. Special Agent Marshall had been openly rooting for Lauren Daniels since the Santa Claus challenge, and Alice knew he'd commiserate with her and her brother. She watched him read the username and recognize the hottie.

"What?" His eyes widened in disbelief. "How could this happen?"

"I have no idea. She's been crushing this contest out of the gate." Alice patted the leather chair beside her own and said, "Here, have a seat. We have to talk this out." As expected, Agent Marshall sat in a chair across the table from Marc instead of in the one she'd offered. Alice didn't comment on the four empty seats between them, but she couldn't help but wonder if the rookie agent kept his distance because of protocol, their six-year age difference, or a mild disdain for his first assignment.

"What's to talk about? Breaking the rules is pretty black and white, correct?" Oliver looked at the photo again and asked, "Which hashtag is this?"

"She's on YOLO." Alice reviewed the timestamp logged with the data and said, "She sent it less than a minute after she got my text."

"Well, that kind of makes sense," Marc said. "The

contest is almost over, and she'd want to hurry. The very nature of 'you only live once' is doing something spontaneous." He pointed to the image on the wall. "Maybe it was on purpose."

"What? No way is she sabotaging herself this close to the finish line." Alice immediately dismissed the idea. "Five bucks says she's kicking herself as we speak."

"Five bucks?" Oliver swiveled in his chair to face Alice. "You'll give ten thousand dollars to a stranger, but make a five-dollar wager with your brother?"

"The five dollars is *my* money. My real money," Alice said. "The ten grand is coming out of the settlement. I'll never spend their money on myself, but it's fun giving it away here and there."

A little more than a year ago, a paparazzi snuck into a private resort and took pictures of Alice drinking underage. Her mother was in the middle of her Presidential campaign, and a tabloid newspaper bought the pictures and featured them on their website. At the time, Alice was a minor, so her family sued the photographer and tabloid. The photos were removed from the site and never published in print. Alice received a substantial amount for damages, but refused to spend the money on herself. After winning the lawsuit, Alice had made several anonymous charitable donations and recently began to develop app-based contests for prize money. It was a fun hobby, and just the distraction she needed while mending a broken heart.

Her last relationship had been heavily dependent on texts, private messages, memes, photos, and links to YouTube and Spotify. They both had busy schedules but had made it work by sprinkling in lunch dates and late-night Snapchats. Alice had become dependent on her smartphone, but not in the way most teens and adults are addicted to their devices. She'd become obsessed with hearing from him, and after months of constant communication and lightning-fast responses, it was a habit to check her phone, knowing she'd have a word from him.

She continued to check long after he had stopped replying, sometimes finding proof that he'd been active in the app and had chosen not to say anything. It made her ache for the days when she'd woken up to a "good morning, beautiful" text with hearts and kissy-face emojis. It wasn't her first breakup, but it was the first one in quite a while. She'd forgotten how it felt to cry herself to sleep at night, heart breaking with her mind reeling. She felt foolish, thinking she'd made up all the parts where the attraction and affection were mutual. With her brother's help, Alice had created the Wizard character and a handful of scavenger hunts. One of her favorite qualities about the contest apps was how they made her phone fun again… and giving away ten thousand dollars never got old.

"This doesn't feel right." Marc had highlighted "@ laurenburger," and Alice knew she was just a cut and paste away from the DQ column. "Can you text her and see if this was a pocket dial type of mistake?"

"That doesn't feel right either," Alice said. "I shouldn't play favorites." She'd been disqualifying contestants left and right for repeating the people and places in their submissions. She checked the time on her phone and said, "Okay, I have an idea."

CHAPTER TWENTY

Lauren

SHE'D NEVER HAD AN OUT-OF-BODY EXPERIENCE, BUT LAUREN couldn't think of any other way to interpret the sensation of hovering above the banquette. Her line of sight had shifted up and to the right, and from this perspective, Lauren watched the events unfold. As if viewing a silent movie with a soundtrack, she could hear the jazz trio in the far corner, but not her friends' voices.

Brenner was kneeling beside Lauren, removing teacup fragments from her shoes. Hazel rushed over to clean, but he stopped her efforts and pointed to the dance floor. She was gone in a flash. She left her bar towel behind, so Brenner sopped up the whiskey as he spoke to Lauren. Floating Lauren wished she could hear what he was telling Frozen Lauren; he was either encouraging her to hang in there or suggesting an effective deep breathing technique. Both possibilities made her smile.

The two couples returned from the dance floor in a hurry, their faces heavy with worry when they saw Frozen Lauren. Brenner had collected the white and yellow china pieces in the bar towel, and he handed the wet bundle to

Hazel before pointing to Lauren's phone on the steamer truck. Floating Lauren watched him pantomime the events the others had missed while dancing.

Ivy snatched up the phone and quickly entered Lauren's passcode. Once the device was unlocked, Ivy tapped on the screen until she saw the photo. The shock on Ivy's face was so undeniable that Floating Lauren half expected her friend's ethereal figure to join her own hovering over the action. She smiled at the idea of a spectral Ivy popping into the air with an incredulous, "Oh, no you diii'int." Down below, Ivy took a teacup off the trunk and slung the whiskey back in one shot. She returned the cup to its matching saucer and passed Lauren's phone to Amy before plopping down in a leather wingback chair.

Amy saw the photo and gasped. It was too easy for Lauren to imagine Amy floating next to Ivy. Without a doubt she'd pretend to be a nervous astronaut and nail her impression of Key and Peele's classic "I Said Bitch" routine. Floating Lauren smiled. Her smile became a giggle that grew into a chuckle...and the laughter within her became so visceral, it burst out of Frozen Lauren's mouth. It was the only noise she'd made since her mistake rendered her mute and immobile, and her sudden liveliness startled her friends. Amy's gasp made Lauren laugh even harder.

"Is she okay?" Amy asked.

"She laughed like this at the hospital," Ivy said. "After the helicopter pictures, she sat on a sofa in the lobby and cracked up. It didn't last long, but it was out of the blue."

"Nervous laughter is a physical reaction to stress," Brenner said. "She doesn't do this usually?"

"I'm okay, I'm okay." The concern in her friends' voices made Lauren return to herself. "I'm laughing so I don't cry," she gasped as she tried to catch her breath. She wiped her eyes dry and said, "I completely blew it, guys. I'm so sorry. It's over."

"Oh, no!" Ivy bolted out of her chair and tackle-hugged Lauren. "I leave you alone for ten minutes…" she teased. She hugged Lauren tighter and asked, "Did they really disqualify you?"

"Probably. I should check." Lauren's phone was still in Amy's hand, and as it was returned to her, Lauren recalled a similar scene from earlier in the contest. Bewildered people in a bar waiting for her to explain why she sent a photo of Brenner to the Wizard. Getting busted in Barkley's felt like it had happened a million years ago, and Lauren smiled at the thought of coming full circle. After a quick glance at her screen, Lauren said, "Nothing yet."

"No news is good news," Ivy declared. "Let's just wait and see."

"Any chance the Wizard won't notice?" asked Moose. "Amy filled me in, but if she's been looking at pictures all night, it might slip by her."

"No chance," said Lauren.

Hazel returned to their table with another round of whiskey, and she brought six thick white mugs this time. "Got one for you too, boss," she said to Moose. Brenner sat on the trunk, Scott and Moose took the leather chairs, and Amy joined Lauren and Ivy on the banquette.

Ivy lifted one of the mugs in the air. "Alright, team, bring it in." Five coffee mugs joined hers with a series of clinks. "To only living once," she said.

"To old friends," Amy added, "and new friends."

"Hear! Hear!" said Moose.

"To the Hashtag Hunt!" Scott raised his mug higher

before tapping the rim of his mug against the others, "Best mission ever!"

"Cheers!" rang out from them all, and they swallowed their shots in unison. As they set their empty mugs on the trunk, Moose signaled to Hazel for another round.

"I'm booking us all a weekend at the spa when this is over," Ivy said.

"Us all?" Scott wiggled his eyebrows at her. "I call dibs on bunking with you."

"I doubt that would be relaxing," Ivy said.

With a flirty wink, he said, "Let's try and see if you're right."

Hazel carried the bottle of whiskey to the table instead of coffee mugs. She handed it to Moose who poured the shots into the mugs himself. "You should be very proud of how far you and your team have come, Lauren. And it sounds like until you get word that you're out, you're still in it."

"I still can't believe I did something so stupid." Lauren jerked her eyes to Brenner and clarified, "Wait! There was nothing stupid about laying one on you. Zero regrets when it comes to kissing you. Smartest thing I've done in a while."

"Glad to hear it," Brenner said with a wink. "And I know what you meant. I only wish I spoke up sooner."

"No, this is all on me." She tossed her phone on the trunk and said, "Being absentminded and trigger-happy was stupid. I was excited about getting the next challenge and wanted to turn it in fast. Surprising Brenner with a kiss seemed like a good YOLO idea at the time, and I'd still have forty-five minutes or so for number twelve."

"Surprising me with kisses is always a good idea,"

Brenner said. "I am sorry it cost you the contest. Out of curiosity, did the Wizard apologize for taking so long with the pay phone picture? I think if you had gotten number eleven in a more timely manner, this could have been avoided."

"Still no word from her, but it's okay," Lauren said. She leaned back in her seat and took a small sip of her whiskey. "Sure, I could use the cash, but I wouldn't trade tonight for anything." She looked at the people gathered around her and said, "I'll never be able to thank you enough. Even you, Moose."

"Oh yeah? How did I help?"

Lauren raised her mug in the air and said, "Whiskey always helps." She kept her eyes on Moose but nodded toward Amy. "And you had an intelligent conversation about the 1920s with this one. I know that made her year."

"It made my *day*," Amy said. "And the sun's not up yet."

"If you say so," crooned Moose. "Impressing you is going to be fun."

"Never lose your optimism, big guy," Amy said with a wink.

Scott pointed to Moose. "My man here invited me to come back to see the other secrets in this building," he said. "My heart may burst: I met a beautiful woman, I have a bowling pin lamp, and there are smuggle spots in this speakeasy."

Ivy left the banquette to sit on Scott's lap. "It was smart to call me beautiful and list me higher than finding that lamp and smuggle spots."

"I am a lot of things, Ms. Ivy, but stupid isn't one of them." Scott tucked her into his side and called to Brenner,

"What about you, B? I know you're glad I dragged you off the couch."

"I am indeed." Brenner twisted around to face Scott and said, "Now that I think about it, your text was the first surprise of many. Of all our missions, this one will always be my favorite."

"Same."

Soon the whiskey and long hours caught up with Lauren, and she yawned loudly. "Excuse me!" she said as she placed her mug back on the table and started to twist the strands of hair that had fallen from her bun.

"Okay, Brenner," Amy said, "here's a little heads-up: when Lauren starts twisting her hair like that, you have maybe thirty minutes before it's lights out."

"Hey!" Lauren sat up straight and dropped the strands of hair from her fingers. "That's not true!"

"Yeah," said Ivy. "It's more like twelve minutes."

Lauren faked outrage and said to Brenner, "I can't believe them."

"I appreciate the helpful hints, ladies," he said to Amy and Ivy. "Keep them coming."

"It goes both ways, you know. I could share some fun facts about you two with Scott and Moose," Lauren said.

As she laughed with her friends, Lauren realized this was the first time since starting the contest that they weren't just killing time until she got the next hashtag. There was no longer a sense of urgency about them, and despite her colossal mistake, Lauren was grateful for this time together. After a fourth and final round of whiskey shots, the couples made their way to the dance floor, and Lauren left her phone behind. Moose and Amy gave lessons on the Charleston and fox-trot, and they laughed and danced until after five in the morning.

Wanting to see if @JayZeeYou or @BertieMags had won the ten thousand dollars, Lauren excused herself from the dance floor. She returned to their table and unlocked her phone. While she knew it was coming, her heart still ached when she saw the Wizard's text on the screen.

Lauren:

Forgive the lengthy text, but there is much to say.

Since you were the only contestant to have submitted an authentic #PayPhone entry at the time, you were in first place when you received the eleventh challenge. I should have disqualified you immediately when the hottie from #HitW was also featured in the #YOLO, but I chose to wait and see how the other players did during the final hour of the contest.

While I will not disclose the details, I can confirm no other contestants submitted an approved #PayPhone picture. An official announcement will come out at noon today, but I'm declaring you the winner of the Hashtag Hunt. If I had disqualified you, I wouldn't have a winner at all. And if I'm being honest: several of your entries blew the competition away, especially the #DumpsterDiveFind, #Helicopter, and #PayPhone photos.

Because it's my contest and I can do what I want, I'm choosing to forget your #YOLO entry ever happened. Cool?

Check your email for instructions on claiming your winnings, and best of luck with everything…especially the hottie!

Congratulations,

The Wizard

Lauren reread the text several times before lifting her eyes from the screen. Brenner was approaching her with a concerned look on his face, and instead of telling him the news, she handed him the phone. He had to scroll up quite a bit to get to the beginning, but once he got the gist, he stood on the steamer trunk, got their friends' attention, and loudly read the Wizard's text to their friends.

Amy and Ivy raced to hug Lauren, and the men waited their turn to offer their congratulations. Instead of stepping down from the trunk, Brenner pulled her up onto its surface and into his embrace. "We keep finding a new 'best surprise,' huh? Each one tops the last."

"I can't believe she let me win the money."

"You deserved it. You got the furthest," Brenner whispered in her ear. He hugged her tighter and said, "I'm so proud of you."

"Couldn't have done it without you. Or them," she said, looking at their friends celebrating around the steamer trunk. She kissed Brenner and then addressed their group. "Celebratory breakfast on me. What do you say?"

"Bar's closed til six, right?" Amy asked Moose. "Can you come with?"

"You bet," he said. "I'll go tell Hazel she's in charge."

Brenner jumped down and offered Lauren a hand. "You ready?" he asked.

"You bet," she answered as she stepped off the trunk. Lauren took the time to kiss him before they headed to the exit. "If this is how we started, I can't wait to see where we go."

He returned her kiss and then said, "Let's go find out."

The End

ACKNOWLEDGMENTS

To Ashley Martin with Twin Tweaks Editing for her enthusiasm for this book and her patience with the rookie who wrote it. Thank you for the support and all you accomplished to transform my little story into a published novel.

To Liam Ashurst for designing my first book cover. I couldn't love it more. Thank you for agreeing to be a part of this project and allowing me to share your illustrative style in this way.

To Stacey Blake with Champagne Book Design, for all the handholding and for turning my boring Word.doc into such a beautiful book! I will never forget seeing your proofs of the book's interior for the first time. I took good notes and will ask fewer questions next time, promise.

To authors Chris Cannon and Casey L. Bond for taking the time to send feedback, advice, and encouragement. Thank you for your friendship, wisdom, and kindness as I wrote my first manuscript.

To my friends who read the earliest versions of *The Hashtag Hunt*: Courtney Murphy, Julie Underwood, Kristin Coke, Tiffany Tomberlin, Sammy Fenton, Martha Parrish, Ana Hayes, Della Albertyn, Jana Barrett, Mandy Smith, Anna Caldwell, Julie Witers, Jennifer Pierce, and Courtney

Carr. Thank you for the honest opinions, for getting the jokes, and for asking when I'd send you the next chapter.

To my favorite paramedic, Katie Currin, for reviewing the scenes involving hospitals, life flight helicopters, and radio communication.

To Christian Aars, Ph.D., and Will Fischer, Ph.D., for their help with star formation…and for requesting "more fiction about smooth-talking astronomers."

To contemporary romance author Tessa Bailey and her Facebook group, Bailey's Babes, for the laughs, swoons, book suggestions, and especially the #HitW sightings.

To my favorite Wizard, Susan Stabley, for the "Selfie Challenge" and its inspiration behind the Hashtag Hunt. Thank you for the decades of friendship, epic Girls' Weekends, and introducing me to Cavalia, Mrs. Wilkes' Dining Room, and Art Basel.

To my #FitFam at Burn Bootcamp in Pineville, NC, for the outpouring of support when I shared my publishing goals. Thank you to Jamie Craft for making BBC much more than a gym (and calling me "Best Seller" during class), the trainers for making the workouts fun (and effective), and my beautiful #BurnSisters for getting it done (and making it look easy).

To my best bae, Lauren Watson, for everything. Thank you for all the ways you have been a wonderful friend to me.

To my parents, Bernie and Jim, for the unconditional love and countless blessings. Thank you for always saying yes when I asked for new books.

To my husband, Ken, for encouraging me every step of this journey. Thank you for the support, patience, and love you shower upon me in so many ways. I am beyond blessed to be your wife.

And to my son, Matt, for telling anyone who will listen that his mom wrote a book. You will always be my greatest accomplishment.

ABOUT THE AUTHOR

Kristina Seek is the marketing and communications director for a residential design-build firm. Sometime near her fortieth birthday, she kicked around the idea of self-publishing a romance novel. With the support of her family and friends, Kristina completed her first book, *The Hashtag Hunt*, in 2018.

Kristina enjoys reading, traveling, and spending time with her loved ones. She lives in North Carolina with her husband and son and is currently writing her second contemporary romance novel.

Connect

Visit www.KristinaSeek.com and sign up for her mailing list to receive updates and exclusive offers!

Follow Kristina Seek on Facebook:
www.facebook.com/KristinaSeekAuthor

and Instagram: www.instagram.com/kristinaseekauthor

Made in the USA
Columbia, SC
01 December 2020